By Phil Bildner

The Rip and Red Series

A Whole New Ballgame
Rookie of the Year
Tournament of Champions
Most Valuable Players

The Sluggers Series
with Loren Long

Magic in the Outfield
Horsin' Around
Great Balls of Fire
Water, Water Everywhere
Blastin' the Blues
Home of the Brave

Most Valuable Players

PhiL BiLDNeR

MostV
PL

pictures by TiM PRoBeRt

aLuaBLe

yers

Farrar Straus Giroux
New York

Farrar Straus Giroux Books for Young Readers
An imprint of Macmillan Publishing Group, LLC
175 Fifth Avenue, New York, NY 10010

1 3 5 7 9 10 8 6 4 2

mackids.com

Library of Congress Cataloging-in-Publication Data

Names:Bildner, Phil, author. | Probert, Tim, illustrator.
Title:Most valuable players: a Rip & Red book / Phil Bildner ; pictures by
    Tim Probert.
Description: First edition. | New York : Farrar Straus Giroux, 2018. |
    Series: Rip and Red ; book 4 | "A Rip and Red Book." | Summary: With their
    fifth-grade graduation only weeks away, Rip, Red, and the rest of their
    classmates must decide if boycotting a test is worth forfeiting their
    graduation gala and the opportunity to play with Hoops Machine,
    a Harlem Globetrotters-like team.
Identifiers: LCCN 2017042498 | ISBN 9780374305109 (hardcover)
Subjects: | CYAC: Best friends—Fiction. | Friendship—Fiction. |
    Basketball—Fiction. | Graduation (School)—Fiction. | Schools—Fiction.
    Autism—Fiction. | African Americans—Fiction.
Classification: LCC PZ7.B4923 Mo 2018 | DDC [Fic]—dc23
LC record available at https://lccn.loc.gov/2017042498

Our books may be purchased in bulk for promotional, educational, or
business use. Please contact your local bookseller or Macmillan Corporate
and Premium Sales Department at (800) 221-7945 ext. 5442 or by e-mail
at MacmillanSpecialMarkets@macmillan.com.

For Mom and Dad,
the Most Valuable Players of all!
—P.B.

For Mary-Kate, Ted, and Alice
—T.P.

Most Valuable Players

Bubba Chuck

Stumbling over her too-big-for-her-body puppy paws, Bubba chased after the flying Frisbee. When it was almost directly overhead, she sprang off her hind legs, leaped as high as she could, and caught it in her mouth.

"Boo-yah!" I shouted from across the backyard.

"Way to go, Bubba Chuck!" Red shook his fists over his head.

My best friend, Red, calls my new dog by her full name. Red calls everyone by their full name. To Red, I'm Mason Irving. To everyone else, I'm Rip.

"Hand," Red called. He knelt by the steps to the deck and held his open palm next to his knee.

As Bubba galloped back across the yard, her floppy ears and the red Frisbee bounced with each stride.

"Release," Red said firmly when she reached him. "Release."

She dropped the Frisbee into his palm.

"Good girl, Bubba Chuck." He rubbed her head. "Good girl."

I'd been asking Mom and Dad for a dog for a gazillion years. Okay, maybe more like *begging* for a dog for a gazillion years, so when Mom took me to the shelter over Easter vacation, I was mind-blown shocked.

Let me tell you, a five-month-old pit bull mix is the best elementary school graduation present of all time. No doubt!

I leaned back on my hands, kicked out my legs, and crossed my feet. "What are you getting for graduation?" I asked Red.

"I don't know." He shrugged.

"Suzanne better hurry up," I said. Suzanne is Red's mom. "She's running out of time."

"She knows what she's getting me," Red said, "but she won't tell me."

I shook out my dreadlocks. "I'll ask her at dinner tonight."

"She won't tell you."

"Maybe she will." I tossed my Philadelphia 76ers mini basketball from hand to hand. "And when she does tell me, I'm going to torture you with the secret."

We were all going out to dinner tonight—me, Red, Mom, Suzanne, and Dana. Mom and Suzanne have been friends for years. Mom and Dana have been dating since the fall.

"You ready, Bubba Chuck?" Red said, shaking the Frisbee.

He pump-faked once, pump-faked again, and then flung it so it rolled on its edge.

Bubba gave chase, but didn't catch up to the Frisbee until it stopped against the chain-link fence in the back of the yard.

"Come, Bubba Chuck!" Red called.

Bubba shook the Frisbee wildly and then charged back across the yard.

"Release," Red said, holding out his hand.

Bubba gave him the Frisbee.

"Sit." Red raised his palm.

Bubba sat instantly.

"Good, Bubba Chuck," Red said. "Shake." He leaned down and held out his hand.

Bubba slapped her paw into it and toppled over.

Red laughed. "Good girl, Bubba Chuck." He fell onto the grass and hugged her.

Red's amazing with Bubba. I knew he would be, because Red's crazy about dogs. But right now, what was even more amazing was seeing Red rolling around on the grass. It was hard to believe he was the same kid who would bug if you even asked him to sit on the ground a few months back.

"Nice job, Dog Whisperer," I said, crawling over.

Red smiled. "I speak the language of puppies," he said.

"I can't believe we're graduating," I said.

"Two weeks from today, Mason Irving," Red said. "Saturday, June 14, at nine o'clock in the morning is graduation. Saturday, June 14, is two weeks from today."

I rolled onto my back and tossed my Sixers ball into the air. "Gala25 is going to be sick."

"Oh, yeah!" he said. "Gala25 is going to be sick!"

Fifth-grade graduation at Reese Jones Elementary is always a big deal, but this year it's an even bigger deal because it's also RJE's twenty-fifth anniversary. Everyone's coming back for Gala25, the huge anniversary party the night before graduation—former teachers, former students, everyone. Both Suzanne and my mom are on the graduation festivities committee, and lots of parents have been busting their butts the last month putting it all together.

"It's so ridiculous they're making us take another test next week," I said.

"So ridiculous, Mason Irving."

I put down the ball and picked at the grass. "It makes no sense," I said. "Who schedules a test on the Wednesday of the last week of school?"

Like most kids in the galaxy, I can't stand standardized tests. This year, testing week was at the beginning of May, and when I finished taking my last one, I was even more relieved than when the dentist told me at my final checkup that it looked like I would never need braces. But then we found out all the fifth and sixth graders in the state have to take this extra test.

Bubba opened her mouth and reached for my Sixers ball.

"Don't even think it, girl," I said. "That's mine."

"No, Bubba Chuck." Red wagged a finger in front of her snoot. "No."

"You want to know what's going to be the best part of middle school?" I said.

"What's going to be the best part of middle school?"

"I won't have to hang around with you anymore."

Red clenched his fists and tapped his legs. "Very funny."

"Ha! I thought so."

"Well . . . well . . . I won't have to hang around with you anymore, Mason Irving."

You may have noticed by now that Red's quirky. Really quirky. He's on the spectrum. Mom and Suzanne have both tried explaining what that means to me more times than I can remember, but I still don't get it, and to be perfectly honest, I'm not sure the grown-ups who say they know what it means know what it means either.

I do know that not everyone gets Red like I do. And not everyone can joke around with him like I can. You also have to explain a lot of things to Red, but once you do, he gets them and remembers them. Red has a crazy-good memory.

He never forgets things like dates or schedules or the lunch menu at school or basketball stats. *Especially* NBA stats. Red loves the NBA.

Not only is Red my best friend, he's also the best friend you can possibly have.

"Did you see the middle school basketball tryouts announcement?" I said. "They're at the end of summer."

"Only two or three sixth graders make the team, Mason Irving."

"I'm going to be one of them," I said, smacking the ball. "No doubt!"

"No doubt!"

I cupped my hand under Bubba's chin and rubbed my nose against hers. "Red and I are going to be in middle school," I said. "Middle school!"

The Stardust Din

"Red's present is a surprise," Suzanne said.

"I won't say anything," I said. "I promise."

"Oh, please, Rip," Mom said. "Everyone
knows you can't keep a secret from Red."

"Yes, I can." I took a breadstick from the bask
it in half. "Don't you understand? I could dri
with this information."

"Thanks a lot, Mason Irving," Red said.

I bumped his shoulder. "That's what best friends are
for."

I'd been trying to convince Suzanne to tell me Red's
graduation present from the moment we sat down at our
booth at the Stardust Diner. I say *our* booth because the
corner booth with the red vinyl cushions next to the old-
fashioned jukebox is where we always sit when we come
here.

"You'll both find out what it is soon enough," Suzanne
said.

"And you won't be disappointed," Dana added.

"You know too?"

"I do." Dana nodded.

To be perfectly honest, I was pretty sure I knew what the present was. Make that, I was almost positive I knew, but I needed confirmation before I could really rub it in Red's face.

I grabbed a blue crayon from the box the hostess had given us and began doodling around the edges of my place mat. Red had started coloring his place mat the second we sat down.

"When was the last time the five of us had dinner together like this?" Suzanne asked.

"I can't remember," Mom said.

"Sunday, April 27," Red said without looking up. "Sunday, April 27, was the last time the five of us had dinner together like this."

"That was the last weekend I had off," Suzanne said. Suzanne's a nurse at a local hospital. "That sounds about right."

"Of course it's right," I said. "Have you ever known Red to forget a date?"

Ding-dong. Ding-dong.

Mom held up her hands. "That's mine," she said, looking at the phones in the middle of the table. "But I'm not getting it."

"You can," Dana said, smiling.

"It'll cost you if you do," I said. "Ha!"

Ding-dong. Ding-dong.

The use of screens is strictly prohibited during mealtime. That's the rule at both our houses. Mom and Suzanne came up with the rule when Red and I got our cell phones for Christmas. At my house, we keep a metal bucket on the kitchen counter. At restaurants, all screens go in the middle of the table. If someone touches one, that person pays for everyone's meal.

The grown-ups have a harder time with the rule than Red and me. Much harder.

Ding-dong. Ding-dong.

"That phone hasn't stopped all week," Mom said. "In fact, that phone hasn't stopped all month. Everyone needs their graduation questions answered now, now, now."

"Everyone's going to have to wait, wait, wait, Rip's Mom," Red said, still coloring. Red calls my mom Rip's Mom. "If not, you're going to have to pay, pay, pay."

We all laughed.

My mom, Lesley Irving, is a middle school principal a few towns over. Every year at this time, she gets crazy busy because she has to organize her school's graduation, and this year she's doubly busy because she has my graduation, too. Even though there are lots of other parents on the graduation festivities committee, they all bounce everything off Mom because they know she's a principal. Everyone thinks she has all the answers.

When it comes to school stuff, she usually does.

"This RJE graduation is going to be extraordinary," Suzanne said.

"No one will be able to say we're not sending you boys out in style," Mom said. "That's for sure."

I thumped my chest. "That's how it should be."

"I'm working doubles all this week and next," Suzanne said. "That way, I have off the entire weekend."

"I have late nights all this week as well." Mom pointed at Red and me. "That means you two need to go easy on us. No last-minute surprises, you hear that?"

"No last-minute surprises," Red said. "I hear that, Rip's Mom."

"I'm serious, you two," Mom added. "The last weeks of school always worry me."

"Is this where you're going to say something about the school board?" I said.

"Don't get me started," Mom said. "The amount of pushback I've gotten from them trying to coordinate the Gala25 festivities is shameful, and . . ." She wagged a finger at me. "I said, don't get me started. And I mean it, no last-minute surprises. Far too often, someone does something I really wish they hadn't, and then I have to spend way too much time cleaning up the mess."

I reached for another breadstick.

"Honey, that's your last one," Mom said. "You won't have any room for your food."

"I always have room for my food."

"Mason Irving always has room, Rip's Mom," Red said.

I do. I eat everything.

"On second thought," Mom said, smiling, "eat all the breadsticks you want. You're going to need extra energy this week."

"Why's that?"

Mom didn't answer.

"Why's that?" I asked again. "What does that mean?"

She kept smiling her I-know-something-you-don't-know smile and didn't respond.

"Which one of you is reading this?" Dana picked up a book from the cushion beside her.

"I'm reading *Giant Steps* by Kareem Abdul-Jabbar," Red said. He stopped coloring. "Kareem Abdul-Jabbar's a basketball player from back in the day."

"I know who he is," Dana said.

"Kareem Abdul-Jabbar wrote *Giant Steps* while he was still playing basketball for the Los Angeles Lakers." Red spun the crayon on the table. "*Giant Steps* is Kareem Abdul-Jabbar's autobiography."

"He's quite an individual," Dana said. "I bet it's fascinating."

"What are you reading?" Suzanne asked me.

I reached behind me for my book. "*The Boys Who Challenged Hitler*. It's a nonfiction book about World War II."

Nonfiction is my favorite genre. Takara Eid is the one who got me hooked. She's this girl who was in our class back in the fall. Everyone called her Tiki. She loved nonfiction and always posted recommendations on the YO! READ THIS! board in our classroom. It's how I learned about *The Boys Who Challenged Hitler*, and it's how Red learned about *Giant Steps*. But Tiki was only in class for a couple months because her family had to move.

"Do you want to know what the sixth graders told us?" Red asked.

"What sixth graders?" Mom said.

"A bunch of sixth graders came to RJE on Friday to speak to us about middle school," Red answered, still spinning the crayon. "They said if you carry a book wherever you go, you'll never get in trouble."

"Is that so?" Mom said.

"It's so, Rip's Mom," Red said. "They said if you're ever somewhere you're not supposed to be, all you need to do is hold up a book and say you were looking for a quiet place to read."

"Is that so?" Mom said again.

"They said in middle school it's good to be known as the kid who's always carrying a book."

"Call me old-fashioned," Mom said, "but I like to think if you carry a book wherever you go, you'll actually read the book."

"If you carry a book wherever you go, you might read it?" I said, pretending to be surprised. "You will? No way!" I grinned and strummed the table. "Two weeks till graduation!"

"Oh, yeah," Red said. "Two weeks till graduation."

"That means there are still two more weeks of school," Mom said.

I shook out my hair. "There are?"

"There most certainly are," Mom said. "And you still have one more test coming up."

"Thanks for reminding us," I said.

"Yeah, thanks for reminding us, Rip's Mom."

"We shouldn't have to remind you," Suzanne added.

"If you ask me," I said, "I think there should be a

constitutional amendment that says you can't give tests the last week of school."

"No one's asking you," Mom said.

I waved my hand. "School's over."

"No, it is not," Mom said. "You need to take that test seriously."

I strummed the table again. "Two weeks till graduation!"

B-Ball in
the Schoolyard

"Irving at the top of the key," I said, announcing the play-by-play. My basketball brain sized up the imaginary defenders. "He goes left . . . blows by his man . . . inside the key . . . puts up the floater . . ."

The shot hit off the back of the rim.

"I need to work on my left," I said, chasing down the rebound and dribbling out to Red at midcourt. "Every time we're out here, we're working on my left."

"You got it, Mason Irving."

Red and I were the only ones in the RJE schoolyard. Mom and Suzanne were both cool with us being here by ourselves on a Sunday afternoon. We both had our cells. We knew to be careful.

I dribbled back and forth between my legs like I was walking in place and then spun away from Red and broke for the corner. A few feet from the baseline, I squared up and took the shot. I banked it in.

"You didn't call glass," Red said.

"I know."

"You have to call glass."

I scooped up the ball and took
a turnaround jumper from
just outside the lane.

Swish!

I needed to hit shots like those if I was going to make the

middle school team, and I was going to make the middle school team.

With my basketball eyes, I checked Red. He was practicing his dribbling, bouncing two balls at once and trying to make like Steph Curry before a game. Every few dribbles, he managed to put the ball between his legs with his left hand and keep the second ball going in front with his right. It looked sick when he did.

"You're getting so much better at that," I said.

"Oh, yeah!" Red basketball-smiled. That's the huge grin he gets when he's playing ball. "Watch this," he said. He trapped one basketball under his foot soccer-style and shot the other.

Air ball.

He laughed and raised his arms. "Sign me up for the NBA All-Star Weekend Three-Point Contest!"

"It would be no contest!" I sat down on my ball, planted my heels, and rolled around.

"I just watched this show on the greatest moments of the NBA All-Star Weekend Three-Point Contest," Red said, sitting down on his ball, too. "Larry Bird of the Boston Celtics won the NBA All-Star Weekend Three-Point Contest three years in a row. Larry Bird was the NBA All-Star Weekend three-point champion in 1986, 1987, and 1988."

"Larry Bird was a beast," I said.

"When Larry Bird won the NBA All-Star Weekend Three-Point Contest in 1988, Larry Bird hit his last three shots. When Larry Bird shot the final red, white, and blue bonus ball, Larry Bird held up his finger as soon as he released it."

"Beast!"

"In the 1991 All-Star Weekend Three-Point Contest," Red went on, "Craig Hodges of the Chicago Bulls hit his first nineteen shots. Nineteen three-pointers in a row, Mason Irving. Nineteen!"

It was time to change the subject. If I didn't, I was going to be hearing about NBA three-point contests for the rest of the afternoon.

"Dunk time?" I said, pointing downcourt.

"Oh, yeah, Mason Irving! Dunk time!"

Over spring break, the school had put up a new basketball hoop, a lower one for the little kids. We're not allowed to dunk on it at recess, but we weren't at recess.

We popped to our feet at the same time and took off downcourt. Red raced ahead, dribbled down the lane, and dunked with two hands.

"Bam!" He hung from the rim.

As soon as he let go, I made my move. I came in from the right, went up with two hands, and threw it down with one.

"Beast!" I thumped my chest. "I'm going to be a beast at middle school tryouts."

"Beast!" Red said.

"I'm not just making the team," I said. "I'm playing for the team. I want to start." I motioned to the far end of court. "Feed me in the corner."

"Sure!"

"I want to take twenty shots," I said as we dribbled back. "Remember to make me use my left."

"You got it."

My basketball brain shifted into offensive mode.

Red threw the first pass.

Catch. Dribble with the left. Set. Shoot.

No good.

Red chased down the rebound and fired the next pass.

Catch. Dribble with the left. Set. Shoot.

Swish!

"Nice, Mason Irving!" Red said.

I missed the next shot, but then I found my stroke and drained four in a row.

"Money!" I said.

"Oh, yeah!" Red started laughing.

"What's so funny?"

"Keep it going, Mason Irving."

"What's so funny?"

Red laughed again. "Keep it going!"

I kept it going. I didn't hit every shot, but I made more than I missed, and when I took the last shot, as soon as I released it, I held up a finger like Larry Bird.

Swish!

"Thirteen out of twenty," Red announced. "That's sixty-five percent. Nice work, Mason Irving."

We topped fists and knocked knuckles.

"What were you laughing about?" I asked.

Red began laughing again.

"What?"

"Avery Goodman," he said.

"What about Avery?"

Avery's a girl from class. At the beginning of the year, I couldn't stand her. Pretty much no one could. But then our teacher, Mr. Acevedo, made us work together on this big group project. Ever since, we've been friends, good friends.

"Avery Goodman says 'money,'" Red said. He picked up the ball. "When Avery Goodman hits her shots, she says 'money.'"

"What shots?" I made a face. "What are you talking about?"

"Avery Goodman started playing wheelchair basketball."

"She did? I thought she wasn't playing until the summer."

Avery has used a wheelchair for as long as we've known her. But she was never into sports until she came to a Clifton United game. That's the name of our basketball team. Now she loves hoops.

"Avery Goodman's awesome!" Red hopped from foot to foot. "You should see Avery Goodman hit shots." He pretended to take a shot. "Money!"

"Why didn't you tell me she started playing?"

"You never asked, Mason Irving."

I swiped the ball from Red. "Five seconds left," I play-by-played as I dribbled for the corner. "Clifton United needs a three to win. Irving with the ball . . . off-balance and falling out of bounds . . . he throws up a prayer . . ."

"OHHHHH!"

Bubba Therapy

"It's on me to up my game," I said. "It's on me, Bubba."

I lay on my bed facing her, rubbing her neck with one hand, propping my head up with the other.

"I can do this," I said. "I know I can. It's just that . . . It's just that almost all the other kids trying out are playing summer league and . . ."

Bubba shifted her head. Her nose pressed against purple teddy's belly.

"Don't even think it." I tossed my fave stuffed animal over my pillow. "That's mine, girl."

I scooched down and placed my head next to hers. Bubba licked my ear.

"That tickles," I said, squirming.

She licked me again.

"Next year is going to be so different," I said. "I'm pumped, but . . . I don't know. It's going to be so many new kids. A part of me doesn't want to go."

I glanced at my journal on the floor. Mr. Acevedo gave me the journal right after I got Bubba. He suggested I write a few sentences about her every day. I did for a little while. I wrote about the first time she rolled onto her back, the first time she saw a vacuum cleaner, the time she tore her bed to shreds, and the time she pooped on the front-door welcome mat instead of on her training pad. Then every time I called Dad, I shared what I'd written. Dad loved hearing the journal entries.

But then I stopped writing in it. I don't know why. I just did. But I still tell Dad all about Bubba. A part of me can't believe he and Mom finally let me get a dog. Dad only has a few months left of his job on the other side of the planet. I can't wait until he's back for good and gets to meet Bubba.

"You know what would be sick?" I said. "If you could spend the day in Room 208. You'd love Mr. Acevedo. He's the coolest teacher I've ever had."

I wiped a booger from the corner of her eye with my thumb. Bubba gets lots of eye boogers.

"But you'd have to promise not to pee on the rug," I said. "And you wouldn't be allowed to sit on the couch or bean-bag chairs. But you would get to see Red."

Bubba's ears shot up.

"Ha!" I said. "You know his name." I rubbed her head. "Bubba Chuck," I said. "Do you like that he calls you Bubba Chuck?"

I did. I loved that Red called her Bubba Chuck.

"Watch this," I said, sliding off the bed. "Here's how Red shoots foul shots."

Bubba stood.

"You stay." I held out my hand. "Stay."

I scooped up the Nerf and sidestepped to where I always take my bedroom free throws. I trapped the ball soccer-style under my left foot and took several breaths. Then I picked up the ball, squared my shoulders, and looked at the front rim. I dribbled three times, spun the ball, extended my arms, and took the underhanded shot.

It clipped the bottom of the rim over my closet.

"Red makes his," I said. "He's a free-throw shooting machine." I dove back onto the bed. "Can I tell you a secret? I haven't even told this to Red. It's . . . it's a little weird."

I let out a puff and placed my hand on her belly.

"You know how . . . I always thought my nickname came from Rip Hamilton, the basketball player? He never stopped running on the court, and that's how I am. But that's not how I got my nickname." I rubbed my eye with my shoulder. "When I was a baby, I used to rip off my diapers and walk around butt naked. That's why I'm Rip."

The Perfect Circle

"L–A–S–T," Mr. Acevedo said at the beginning of class Monday morning. "We're going to have lots of lasts this week and next. Our last lunch, our last recess, our last Genius Hour for independent study, our last—"

"Pee in the bathroom!" Diego called out.

Everyone laughed.

"Thanks, Diego." Mr. Acevedo hopped off the beanbag chair he'd been standing on and stood in the middle of the meeting-area rug. "These are your last days at RJE and my last days as a first-year teacher."

"Are you finally going to tell us your plans for next year?" Attie asked.

"Nope," he said.

"But you told us you would," Melissa said.

"And I will."

Way back on the second day of school, Mr. Acevedo had told us he only had a one-year contract at RJE. Whenever we asked him about his plans for next year, he wouldn't say. But he did say he'd let us know before we graduated.

He was running out of days.

"Is Ms. Hamburger un-retiring and replacing you?" Attie said.

"Ms. Hamburger's coming back?" Hunter asked.

"Whoa, whoa, whoa," Mr. Acevedo said, chuckling. "I can assure you that's not happening."

Ms. Hamburger was supposed to be our teacher this year. Up until this year, she'd been the only fifth-grade teacher RJE ever had. But right before the start of school, she announced her retirement. Mr. Acevedo took her place.

"Do you know what your plans are for next year?" Xander asked.

"We're working on them, X," Mr. Acevedo said. He brushed some hair off his face. "Now I'm giving everyone a warning. I will get sentimental these last days. Guaranteed. And if you don't know what *sentimental* means, look it up."

I knew what *sentimental* meant. It's how Mom gets when she's relocking my hair and telling me stories about when I was little. Like how when I was four, I climbed out the bathroom window so I could chase the garbage truck down the street. I used to love to chase the garbage truck.

"We'll have most of class outside this morning," Mr. Acevedo said. "It's a beautiful day, and we have a fantastic book to finish for Teacher's Theater Time. But before we head out to the amphitheater for T3, I want to share the Voices Beyond I'll be posting later."

Voices Beyond is our class blog. Mr. Acevedo is a big fan of student voice. He's always telling us how what we have to say has value and matters, and how it's important to share our words and thoughts beyond Room 208. Mr. Acevedo also thinks it's important we listen to what other students elsewhere have to say. Whenever he hears about a fifth grader doing something meaningful from his Voxer group—Mr. Acevedo's in a Voxer group chat with a bunch of fifth-grade teachers from all around the country—he posts about it in Voices Beyond.

Mr. Acevedo worked the whiteboard and pulled up a video.

"This young lady used only a green screen and her Galaxy for this project," he said. "It's brilliant."

A girl who looked a lot like Attie (but who wasn't Attie) sat behind a news anchor desk and gave a report on climate change. At one point, she interviewed a man wearing a suit and a hard hat (who had to be her father, because they looked

▷ ▷| ⊲))) 00:05 / 00:12 ⚙ [ ]

so much alike) in front of a power plant with steam rising out of the cooling towers.

"We celebrate our voices in Room 208," Mr. Acevedo said when the video ended. "We share our book recommendations. We share our best efforts." He motioned to the YO! READ THIS! board in one back corner and the Swag board in the other. "We share a part of ourselves."

He finger-drew a circle around us in the air.

"What can we do to improve the chances our voices will be heard beyond these four walls?" Mr. Acevedo nodded to the paused video. "That was creative. How else can we be creative? What are some other ways we can amplify our voices?"

He drew another circle in the air.

"On your own, think about—"

"Oh, yeah!" Red shouted. He leaped out of his seat—accidentally knocking over his chair—and pointed at Mr. Acevedo. "Holy bagumba!"

Everyone laughed.

Red looked around, and suddenly the excitement on his face disappeared. His hands began shaking. He hunched his shoulders and bent his knees. Then he covered his eyes and pressed his chin to his chest and his elbows to his sides.

Red doesn't like it when people stare and laugh at him. I don't think anyone does, but Red really doesn't like it. He was having an episode. I couldn't remember the last time he'd had one. He used to bug like this all the time, but not anymore, and never out of nowhere.

This had come from out of nowhere.

"Red?" I stood and placed my hand on his back. I could feel how hard he was breathing. "Red, you okay?"

I glanced at Mr. Acevedo. I could tell he had no clue what had brought this on either. And Ms. Yvonne, the special ed teacher who worked with Red, wasn't in the room this morning.

"Red, what is it?" I moved my hand to his shoulder and gave a soft squeeze.

"What happened, Red?" Mr. Acevedo knelt in front of him. "Let us help you."

I felt his breathing slow.

"We got you, Red," I said. "It's all good."

Red inched his trembling hands from his eyes and slowly unbent his knees.

"It's all good, Red," Mr. Acevedo said. He put one hand on Red's calf and picked up the chair with his other. "Take your time."

Red clenched his fists and held them to his chest. "I'm okay," he whispered. His knuckles knocked. "I'm okay."

"Take your time, Red," I said. I slid my hand to the back of his head. "We got you."

"I'm okay." Red loosened his shoulders. "I'm okay."

Mr. Acevedo stood back up. "What can we do for you, Red?" he asked.

"Do that again, Mr. Acevedo," Red said softly.

"Do what again?"

"With your finger."

"I don't understand." Mr. Acevedo glanced at me. "What do you want me to do?"

Red's fists now tapped his legs. "Draw the circle," he said.

"You want me to do this?" Mr. Acevedo drew another circle around us.

Red smiled and nodded.

Mr. Acevedo drew another.

"I knew it," Red said.

"Knew what, Red?" Mr. Acevedo started to smile.

"The circle." Red slid back into his chair.

I sat down too. "What about the circle?"

"You noticed, Red?" Mr. Acevedo said.

"Noticed what?" I looked from Red to Mr. Acevedo. "What am I missing?"

Red bounced in his seat. His knees knocked against the underside of our table. "Mr. Acevedo draws a perfect circle with his finger," he said.

"Finally!" Mr. Acevedo raised both arms. "Yes!"

"What are you two talking about?" I said.

"Mr. Acevedo draws a perfect circle in the air with his finger," Red said.

"Yes!" Mr. Acevedo raced to the front of the room and hopped onto the table where Olivia, Mariam, and Grace (aka the OMG girls) were sitting. "You're the first person to notice, Red. Well done!"

"Thanks, Mr. Acevedo." Red bounced faster.

"Right now," Mr. Acevedo said, waving his hands, "everyone should be imagining balloons and streamers and confetti falling from the ceiling. We have a winner!"

"We have a winner!" Red cheered.

Everyone clapped.

"Dude," Avery said, rolling to Red and hockey-stopping next to him. "Great catch."

"Thanks, Avery Goodman."

"I'll say," Trinity said. "Good job, Red. G-O-O-D J-O-B, good job!"

Red laughed. "Thanks, Trinity Webster."

"I can't believe no one noticed until now," Mr. Acevedo said, drawing another circle. "I thought for sure one of you would have."

"How do you do it, Mr. A.?" Danny asked.

"Ah." Mr. Acevedo wagged the finger. "A magician never reveals his secrets."

"Then how do we know it's a perfect circle, Teach?" Declan said.

"You doubting me?" Mr. Acevedo made a fake-insulted face and jumped down. "It's a perfect circle. Guaranteed."

"We'd like to see some evidence, Mr. A.," Attie said.

"Evidence?" Mr. Acevedo backpedaled to the board and motioned to the pen tray. "Pick a color, Red," he said.

"Red!" My best friend popped back to his feet.

Mr. Acevedo picked up the red marker. With his thumb and index finger, he held it out to the class and flicked it back and forth. Then he tucked his hair behind his ears and Michael-Jackson-toe-turned to the board. He raised the marker over his head and pinched the back of his elbow like he was fastening the joint. He straight-arm-lowered the marker and touched the top of the board, the middle of the board, and the bottom of the board.

"Here we go," Mr. Acevedo said.

He drew a perfect red circle on the whiteboard.

Room 208 cheered.

"We have a winner!" Mr. Acevedo pointed the marker at Red.

"We have a winner!" Red hopped from foot to foot. "What did I win, Mr. Acevedo?"

"Your prize?" Mr. Acevedo wrapped his thumb and index finger around his chin. "Good question." He thought for a moment. "Your prize is, you get to keep all the novels we read in T3 this year."

"Oh, yeah!" Red said. "Thanks, Mr. Acevedo."

Sentimental

Mr. Acevedo walked the benches of the Amp—the sitting area at the swing-set end of the playground—as he read from *The Great Greene Heist*. Every so often, he would pause or throw up his hand or turn quickly or hop into the air.

Teacher's Theater Time.

I thought back to the very first T3. I pictured Mr. Acevedo sliding and gliding around our seats and then leaping and bouncing from table to table as he read *Lawn Boy*. I couldn't believe my eyes. I couldn't believe my ears. No teacher had ever read to any of my classes like that.

I thought about the time he read *How to Steal a Dog* and the way he read the different voices—Georgina, Mama, Toby. I felt like I was in Darby right along with them. We all did.

I checked Red. He sat in his usual T3-in-the-Amp spot at the end of the front bench next to Mr. Goldberg.

Mr. Goldberg's the head custodian at RJE. Whenever we have T3 in the Amp, he always joins us. I thought back to the first time he did. It was the day Mr. Acevedo read us the James Howe short story about the kid with the same first and last name. I loved that story.

I looked down my row to Diego. He lay on his back with his legs in the air like he was pedaling a bicycle. In third and fourth grade, Diego had been sick. Like, really sick. Like, almost-died sick. He used to wear hats because the medicines he took made his hair fall out. But not anymore. He's all better now. He was even able to play for Clifton United in a tournament during Easter.

I peeked over at Avery, sitting on the bench. Avery was getting out of her chair more and more now. She always got out of her chair for T3 in the Amp.

I gazed up at Mr. Acevedo and gripped the back of my neck. Would my middle school ELA teacher read to us like this? Would my middle school ELA teacher read to us at all?

The Basketball Equation

I behind-the-back-tossed the balled-up tinfoil into the trash, waved to Ms. Arnett and Ms. Jergensen—the two first-grade teachers on lunch duty—and bolted out of the cafeteria. I tore down the hall.

"No running, Rip," Ms. Waldon said.

"Hey, Ms. Waldon," I said.

Ms. Waldon's the parent coordinator who sits at the desk under the announcement monitor in the main hall. She's the eyes and ears of RJE.

"Slow down," she said. "No getting hurt these last two weeks."

"No getting hurt," I said, finger-flicking the clipboards hooked to the front of her desk as I speed-walked by. "I promise."

I turned the corner at the end of the hall and sprinted for the stairs.

A few minutes before, on the way down to lunch, Mr. Acevedo had told me he wanted to speak with me and that I should come back to the room when I finished eating. So I inhaled my fish tacos (I think they were fish tacos) as fast as I could.

I two-at-a-timed the steps and bounded onto the second floor. I pretend-dribbled as I raced down the hall, and when I got to Room 208, I smacked the top of the door frame like I was smacking a backboard—not that I'm able to come anywhere close to smacking a real backboard.

"Hey, Mr. A." I dove onto the beanbag chair closest to the door.

"Thanks for coming up, Rip," he said. Mr. Acevedo sat cross-legged on the front table, reading. He bookmarked his page and closed the book. "I promise I won't keep you long. I don't want you missing recess."

"I'm not in trouble, am I?" I asked.

"Not unless you've done something I don't know about," he said. He swung his legs off the table and headed for the board. "This is a good thing."

I clasped my hands behind my head and leaned back against the couch as Mr. Acevedo worked the board and punched up an equation.

"What's that?" I said.

"A sneak preview of the last equation I'm sharing with the class."

"That's what you wanted to tell me? Are you going to show me a bonus *mi abuela* quote, too?"

"You're a funny guy, Rip."

Mr. Acevedo's family is Dominican. At the beginning of the school year, he always shared with the class things his grandmother used to say to him. He called them his *mi abuela* quotes. But by December, he'd run out of them. So he started sharing word equations instead. My favorite was the very first one:

Mathematics of Life
$$\text{Life} + \text{Laughter} \times \text{Love} - \text{Hate} = \text{Happiness}$$

I popped off the beanbag chair and sat on the front table in the spot where Mr. Acevedo had been reading when I walked in.

"I made a little Prezi for you," he said, pressing Play. "Luck." He spoke like a narrator as the word appeared in all caps in the middle of the board. "What is luck? Luck is what happens when preparation meets opportunity."

The word *Luck* faded, and two huge emoji fists appeared. The fist on the left had *Preparation* in typewriter font across the knuckles. The fist on the right had *Opportunity*. As the fists came together, the fingers unfolded, and the hands shook.

"We create our own luck," Mr. Acevedo said. "We nurture

it, too. When we do—when preparation and opportunity come together—we seize the moment."

The *Os* in the word *Opportunity* turned into basketballs as the two words faded. Then the basketballs became the *Os* in the words *Hoops Machine*.

"Your luck moment has arrived, Rip," Mr. Acevedo said. He tapped the board. "You ever hear of these guys?"

"Hoops Machine? Of course!"

If you know anything about basketball, you know Hoops Machine. They're this Harlem Globetrotters–like team that performs all over the world. Some of the tricks they do and some of the shots they make are ridiculous. They're hilarious, too.

Mr. Acevedo clicked off the presentation and headed for the meeting area. I rolled off the table, hurdled the beanbags, and Superman-ed onto the couch.

"What's up with Hoops Machine?" I asked.

Mr. Acevedo sat on the lip of the bathtub (yes, our classroom meeting area has a bathtub). "Hoops Machine's coming to Gala25."

"Seriously?"

"Seriously. They're performing at the high school before the dance."

"Yes!" I hammer-fisted the air. "That's the sickest . . . That's the sickest thing in the history of ever!"

"Here's the part you're really going to like." He tapped my knee with a finger. "You're playing with Hoops Machine."

"Don't kid, Mr. Acevedo."

"I'm not kidding, Rip. You're going to be out there playing with Hoops Machine."

"How?" I shook out my dreads and crazy-waved my hands in front of my face. "Why? How?"

Mr. Acevedo chuckled. "I was asked to suggest a player from Clifton United," he said. Mr. Acevedo also coached our basketball team. "I suggested you."

"Boo-yah!" I leaped off the couch and hammer-fisted the air again. "Thanks, Mr. Acevedo!"

"Well, here's the catch," he said.

I froze. "Uh-oh."

"The first practice is this evening."

"No!" I grabbed my head. "I have no way of getting there. My mom has to work late this week, and I—"

"It's all taken care of," Mr. Acevedo said, cutting me off. "Lesley and I worked it out over the weekend."

"My mom knows?"

"She can take you to practice."

"I can't believe she didn't say anything."

My brain flashed back to the Stardust Diner the other night. That's why she said I would need extra energy this week. That's why she smiled her I-know-something-you-don't-know smile.

"Make sure you thank her," Mr. Acevedo said. "She's really going out of her way for you tonight."

"Yes, yes, yes!" I pounded the couch cushions. "Thank you, thank you, thank you!"

"You will have to keep this under wraps," he said.

"I can't say anything?"

"Not yet." Mr. Acevedo shook his head. "It's going to be tough keeping Hoops Machine a surprise. Too many people know about it already. But we should be able to keep *you* a surprise."

"Yes, yes, yes!" I stomped my feet and punched my thighs. "This is unbelievable! Can I tell Red?"

"I'd really rather you hold off. Like I said, we want this—"

"I won't tell anyone else. You know I won't."

Pumped

"Someone's a little excited," Mom said.

"I'm playing with Hoops Machine!" I said, bongo-drumming the dashboard. "I'm going to be on the same court as Hoops Machine!"

We were on our way to the practice at the community college. I'd spent the whole ride messing with my basketball—spinning it on my finger, passing it from knee to knee, rolling it around under my feet, and hugging it.

Yeah, I was a little excited.

"I still can't believe you didn't tell me," I said, staring up at the red light by the campus entrance and wishing it green.

"Honey, I didn't want to say anything until I knew I could make it work."

"But once you did know, you still didn't say anything."

"No," Mom said, smiling. "I guess I didn't."

"Does Dad know?" I asked.

"Not yet," Mom said. "I thought you'd want to tell him. You'll FaceTime with him later."

The light turned. I squeezed the basketball and bounced in my seat.

"Honey, calm down."

"Not possible."

"You can sit still, Rip."

"Not happening." I squeezed the ball harder, but bounced slower.

"You sure you don't want me to come in with you?" she asked.

"Mom, I'm sure."

"I want to play with Hoops Machine, too," Mom said, smiling. She nudged me with an elbow. "I still got game, you know. More game than you, in fact. I think I should be the one who—"

"I'm playing with Hoops Machine!"

"Just remember, when you get inside—"

"I know, I know," I said. "I'll wave to let you know everyone's in there, and I'll text when there's a half hour left of practice."

Mom must've reminded me of that a gazillion times on the way over. Okay, maybe not a gazillion, but she'd said it a lot, and I'd heard her the first time. Well, to be perfectly honest, it was probably the second time or third time.

We turned into the parking lot.

"You'll be at Perky's?" I said.

"I will."

"You do know we just passed, like, three coffee places, right?"

"I know."

"I bet they're less expensive." I nudged her with my elbow.

Perky's was Mom's favorite coffee shop. She always complained about how ridiculously overpriced it was, but that never stopped her from going. Dana liked going there, too. I loved their killer cheesecake brownies.

"It's only a twenty-five-minute drive," Mom said. "Less if the traffic gods are playing nice. And Dana's already there waiting for me. She's knee-deep in her graduation planning, and I have plenty of Gala25 e-mails to send out. Honey, you should see this guest list. It's like the who's who of RJE, past and present. Ms. Wright, Ms. Hamburger, the Lunch . . . You're not listening to a word I'm saying, are you?"

I stared at her. "I'm playing with Hoops Machine!" I stomped my feet. "I'm playing with Hoops Machine!"

She pulled up to the curb by the athletic center.

"Honey, you're sure—"

"Mom."

"Okay." She lifted her hands off the wheel. "Have fun."

"No doubt!" I kissed her cheek. "Thanks for bringing me. I love you, Mom."

Meeting the Machine

"You must be Mason Irving."

Ruiz was jogging toward me. Anyone who knew anything about Hoops Machine knew Ruiz.

"I am," I said.

She held out both hands.

I slid the bag off my shoulder and passed her my ball.
She caught it with her right
hand and then, in one motion,
swung the ball around her back
and bounced it through
her legs to her left.

"What's good, what's
good?" she said. "I'm
Ruiz."

We arm-wrestle-shook
hands and bumped shoul-
ders.

On Hoops Machine, Ruiz ran the show. Red always compared her to Meadowlark Lemon on the old Harlem Globetrotters. The first time he did, I had to YouTube Meadowlark Lemon. Five seconds into the first vid, I knew exactly what he meant.

Red still didn't know I was playing with Hoops Machine. I'd had plenty of chances to tell him at school, but I decided this was the kind of news I needed to share with him alone, because Red was going to bug. Seriously bug.

"Charlie Roth said you like to be called Rip," Ruiz said, thumbing the court.

"Charlie Roth's here? Mega-Man?"

"Mega-Man, Mega-Man." Ruiz squeezed the basketball. "That's what he said he wanted to be called." She spun around. "Mega-Man!"

I knew Mega-Man from when he played for Clifton United in the tournament over Easter. But before then, before I got to know him, I couldn't stand him. No one on our team could. During fall ball, he'd played for Millwood, and in one game, he elbowed our best scorer in the head and knocked him out of the game.

We hated everyone on Millwood, especially their coach. We called him Coach Crazy because he was out of control. Red was absolutely terrified of the guy. In that game where

Mega-Man hurt our player, Coach Crazy tried picking on Red, but Red ended up showing him who was boss.

The thing is, Coach Crazy turned out to be Mega-Man's dad. We had no idea until Mega-Man played for us, and a few weeks ago, Mom told me that Coach Crazy had a heart attack. This was the first time I'd seen Mega-Man since.

"I didn't know you were going to be here," Mega-Man said, walking up.

"I didn't know *you* were going to be here."

We topped fists. Our eyes met. He knew I was thinking about his dad. I was sure of it.

"Um, I . . . I need to let my mom know I found you," I said, turning to Ruiz and motioning to the doors.

"For sure, for sure," Ruiz said. "Always listen to your moms."

"Back in a sec!"

* * *

"Here's how we do," Ruiz said, when I got back to the gym. "A week from Saturday, we performing our Family Fun Night Exhibition. It's the condensed, faster-paced version of our full show. The performance runs fifty-seven to sixty-two minutes."

Ruiz spoke like she was reciting a speech.

"For our Family Fun Night Exhibition," she went on, "we invite a guest to join us on the floor. A week from Saturday, we inviting two." She pointed at Mega-Man and me. "Between now and then, we gots four practices. But the next one isn't until Sunday because we all booked this week. Four practices to get this down." She flipped me my ball. "You with me so far?"

Mega-Man nodded.

I basketball-smiled like Red.

"All our Family Fun Night Exhibitions be the same," Ruiz said, "but no two performances ever be identical. That's what keeps us sharp out there. Keeps us focused, keeps us focused." She looked from me to Mega-Man. "We good?"

"We good," I said, surprised I was able to form words through my mega-grin.

Ruiz arm-wrestle-shook hands and bumped shoulders with Mega-Man. Then she arm-wrestle-shook hands and bumped shoulders with me. For less than a nanosecond, we locked eyes.

"We good, we good," Ruiz said. "We break our Family Fun Night Exhibitions into seven segments: the opening routine, the player introductions." She counted fingers. "The team scrimmage, the HM Flyers, the community scrimmage, the closing routine, the finale. Seven segments." She held up her fingers. "Got that, got that?"

"Got it." I tapped my temple.

Ruiz motioned to the court. "That's everyone," she said. "Groll, Croft, Wicks, Gersh, Sinanis, Bailey, Skeggs, Bray, Rekate. Arnold and Peskin will be here next practice. We on a last-name basis here."

My basketball brain churned.

"Got it all," I said.

"Got what all?" Ruiz said.

"Names, faces, and numbers," I said. I tapped my temple again. "Got it all."

Ruiz nodded once. "Okay, then."

With my basketball eyes I spotted Croft, spinning and stopping and moving in every direction in his wheelchair. I loved watching his vids online, but seeing him doing the moves in person was next level.

"When I'm in my flow," he liked to say in his videos, "I become one with my ride. My chair becomes an extension of my body. My brain is connected to my vehicle."

My mind shot to Avery. She had to be out here, too. Hoops Machine needed to invite *three* guests a week from Saturday.

"The closing routine, the closing routine," Ruiz said. "You two know about it?"

I high-step-danced to the right and high-step-danced to the left. Then I flipped the ball to Mega-Man, crossed my right foot over my left, and spun a three-sixty.

For the closing routine, Hoops Machine danced their own version of the Electric Slide. Everyone in the audience joined in. I've danced it a gazillion times in my bedroom.

"Looking good, looking good, Hoops Skywalker," Ruiz said.

Hoops Skywalker.

My mega-grin returned. If Hoops Skywalker became my nickname, that would be the sickest nickname. No doubt!

Ruiz turned to Mega-Man. "You performing with the HM Flyers."

"I get to dunk?" he said, pointing to himself.

"We see how you do first," Ruiz said.

The HM Flyers were the Hoops Machine basketball aerialists.

"Do I get to dunk?" I asked, jumping up and down. "At the trampoline park, I can—"

"You in the opening number." Ruiz took my ball from Mega-Man and underhanded it to me.

"Sweet." I dribbled back and forth behind my back.

"Both of you play in the community scrimmage," Ruiz said. "After the first basket, we have a dance routine. We'll teach you it before we leave today and . . ."

I raised my knee, shook my leg like Michael Jackson, and did another three-sixty spin. Then I shook my shoulders and did the zombie moves from "Thriller."

"Okay, then," Ruiz said.

Suddenly, Mr. Acevedo's equation flashed inside my head.

Luck = Preparation + Opportunity.

Mr. Acevedo had picked me for this opportunity. He knew

I was prepared. Next week, I was going to be out there in front of everyone, performing with Hoops Machine at Gala25. I was going to create my luck.

"Enough talk, enough talk," Ruiz said. "Let's go play some basketball."

Dream Team

You know when someone says they have to pinch themselves to make sure they're awake? Well, I'd never done that. Until right then. I mean, I knew I was awake, and I knew this was really happening, but if ever there was a time to make extra, extra, extra sure, this was the time.

I was playing basketball with Hoops Machine. I was standing in a circle in the middle of a basketball court with Ruiz, Skeggs, Croft, Sinanis, Rekate, Bailey, and Groll.

"Go, go, go!" Ruiz called.

Three basketballs started flying back and forth across the circle.

"Catch 'em, catch 'em, catch 'em!" Ruiz chanted.

If Clifton United or any other team I ever played for tried whipping rapid-fire chest passes like this, the balls would've knocked into each other and at least one kid would've been doinked in the face by the second or third throw.

Hoops Machine fired their passes with pinpoint precision.

The first pass that came my way was from Bailey. I caught it clean and sent it right off to Skeggs, but before I could reset my hands, Groll's pass was coming at me. I caught that one clean, too, and fired it to Croft.

"Catch 'em, catch 'em, catch 'em!" Ruiz sang.

I was in full-throttle basketball mode and beaming. How could I not be?

"Time, time, time," Ruiz said after about a minute of perfect passing. "Well done, well done." She dribbled middle and faced me. "Hoops Skywalker got skills."

Hoops Skywalker. The nickname was sticking.

"You can stop smiling now, kid." Groll elbowed me.

"No, I can't," I said, shaking my head. "I really can't."

Hoops Machine laughed.

"When that opening music starts," Ruiz said, still facing me, "we all dance out into our circle. We do our bits, crack our jokes, get the laughs, and—"

"I know all the parts," I said.

"Okay, then," Ruiz said.

I clapped for the ball. Ruiz underhanded it to me. I slide-stepped to Sinanis and started behind-the-back passing the ball over my shoulder to myself. Just like he did during the opening.

"Looking good," Sinanis said.

I backpedaled across the circle, dropped to the floor, and butt-spun to Rekate. Then I began dribbling-while-seated like she did during the opening. I tried doing her sick crossover—the one I'm sure she can do in her sleep—but I lost the handle.

"Work," Rekate said. "You'll get it."

I flipped the ball up to Ruiz and sprang to my feet. Then I crow-hopped over to Bailey and began dancing the Carlton the way he does during the opening.

Bailey danced along.

Everyone laughed.

"Spinners, spinners, spinners!" Ruiz called.

In a flash, the three balls went to Skeggs, Sinanis, and Croft. They each spun their ball on their fingers and then rolled it across their chests and up and down their arms. My eyes were glued on Croft as he rocked and shifted in his chair and moved the ball around his body.

"Aight, here we go!" Groll announced. "Motion!"

Croft poked his spinning ball into the air, shoulder-passed it to Groll, and then, pumping both rims, took off downcourt. Groll led him with a pass that Croft caught with one hand. He dribbled once and then whipped the ball off the backboard for Bailey, who was tailing him down the floor. Bailey leaped high into the air, caught the ball, and threw it back against the board. Then the rest of Hoops Machine followed. One by one, we midair-caught the passes and threw them off the backboard. I caught Rekate's throw. Ruiz caught mine. Groll caught the last one and finished the set with an arched-back, full-extension monster slam.

"That's what I'm talking about!" Groll thumped his chest.

"Boo-yah!" I hammer-fisted the air.

"Boo-yah!" Bailey imitated me.

Everyone laughed.

"Why do peeps calls you Rip?" Rekate asked.

I swallowed. "Um, because—"

"After Rip Hamilton?" she said before I could answer.

"Yeah." I nodded. "After Rip Hamilton."

Peeps did call me Rip after Rip Hamilton. Even though I wasn't Rip after Rip Hamilton. I was Rip because I used to rip off my diapers, but peeps didn't know that. Peeps didn't need to know that.

"I can see why they do," Rekate said. "You're on all cylinders out here."

I shook out my dreads and scooted next to Skeggs. "I got a handshake," I said.

"Let's see what you got," she said.

"My friend Red and I made it up."

A few seconds later, Skeggs and I were rolling our arms and dancing, slapping our hands, jumping hip-bumping, and then shouting, "Boo-yah!"

"Hoops Skywalker putting on a show," Ruiz said.

"Man, I like this kid already," Groll added.

"Let's go, let's go." Ruiz clapped twice and pointed to the court. "Back to the circle."

As I bolted to my spot, my basketball eyes checked the door to the auxiliary gym. That's where Mega-Man was practicing with the HM Flyers. I could see the mini trampolines set up around one of the hoops. I wondered if he was getting to dunk. I wanted to so badly.

"Handlers, handlers, handlers!" Ruiz called.

In a flash, the balls went to Groll, Bailey, and me.

Yeah, me.

"Let's see what you got," Skeggs said.

"Show us your stuff, Jedi," Croft added.

I dribbled back and forth between my legs like I was walking in place. Then I dribbled behind my back, right to left and left to right.

"Work," Rekate said.

"Everyone's going to be watching you, watching you," Ruiz said. "You gonna mess up, Hoops Skywalker?"

I kept on dribbling and kept on smiling.

"All eyes on you, Jedi," Croft said.

"No pressure, kid," Groll said.

Luck = Preparation + Opportunity.

"Look at Irving handle that rock," I announced. "You'd think he'd been playing with Hoops Machine all his life. Oh, what a crossover!"

"What are you doing?" Bailey asked.

"The play-by-play," I said. "I like calling the action when I play."

Groll laughed. "Man, I like this kid a lot!"

"I say we switch things up at the beginning," Skeggs said. "Since our guest can ball, let's give him a bigger role."

"I like the way that sounds," I said.

"Can we get him a uniform?" Skeggs asked Ruiz.

"Can do, can do," she said.

I smacked the ball. "I love the way this sounds."

"We'll have Rip be our latecomer," Skeggs said. "He'll

wear the uniform under his clothes, and after we mess with him, he'll flip the script on us."

"Sweet!" I said.

I knew exactly what Skeggs was talking about. During the opening number, if someone in the audience walked in late, they pulled the person onto the floor and made him or her dance or do push-ups and things like that.

"We'll have you and a few of your friends sit down front at one end of the bleachers," Skeggs said to me. "After we start, you'll get up and walk along the sideline toward the middle. We'll make like you're the latecomer and drag you onto the court."

I hammer-fisted the air.

"We should make an intro for him," Sinanis said.

"Now introducing," Groll said, cupping his hands around his mouth and speaking like an announcer, "the newest member of Hoops Machine, out of . . . what school do you go to?"

"Reese Jones Elementary."

"Out of Reese Jones Elementary," Groll continued, "wearing number . . . what's your number?"

"Thirty-two."

"No, it isn't." Sinanis wagged his finger. "That's my number."

"Twenty-four," I said. "That's my friend Red's favorite

number." I looked at Skeggs. "The one I made the handshake with."

My brain bounced to Red. Yeah, he was going to bug like he'd never bugged before when he found out Hoops Machine was coming to Gala25 *and* I was playing with Hoops Machine. Red had to be out here, too. Hoops Machine needed to invite *four* guests. That would be sick!

"You should see Red shoot free throws," I said. "He's a beast from the line. I've seen him make thirty in a row. Forty!"

"Good to know, good to know," Ruiz said.

Red was going to spontaneously combust when I told him I was talking to Hoops Machine about him!

"I'm digging the way you seizing the moment, Hoops Skywalker," Ruiz said.

"Thanks," I said. "I still can't believe I'm getting to—"

"Believe, believe." She rested her arm on my shoulder the way my friend Diego sometimes does. "Always believe. You do on the court. We all see it."

"Thanks," I said again.

"Experiences like this change the trajectory of your basketball life," she said. "They do, they do. And they can also change the trajectory of your entire life, if you allow it." She lifted her arm and tapped the back of my head. "Now I'mma say something to you I've only said to a handful of other guests. You listening?"

"I'm listening," I said.

"My moms teaches middle school," Ruiz said.

"Your mom's a teacher?"

"Middle school math and science for the last twenty-seven years. I visit her classes all the time, all the time. Talk about the math and science of ball." Ruiz moved in front of me. "I know my middle schoolers, Jedi. I spot the good ones when they come along. You're one of the good ones."

I nodded.

"Trust your instincts," she said. "Off the court as much as you do on the court. Follow that heart of yours. You know what's right." She tapped the back of my head again. "You know who you are, Rip. Be who you are. Be true."

Lab Rats

"Let's get this out of the way," Mr. Acevedo said. "Let's talk about next week."

We started class the following morning with Community Circle, CC. We met in the meeting area like we always do; Mr. Acevedo sat cross-legged on the rug in his usual spot.

"This is the only time we're talking about next Wednesday's T-word," he said. "We're not spending our last days of fifth grade focused on it."

The T-word is *test*. We're not permitted to say the T-word in Room 208.

"You couldn't have discussed this yesterday when I wasn't here?" Ms. Yvonne said, smiling. She sat on the couch between Hunter and Attie. "I wouldn't have minded."

"We didn't want you to miss out," Mr. Acevedo said, strumming his legs. "It's good to have you back."

"It's good to be back," she said. "It's about time."

Ms. Yvonne is the special ed teacher who pushes into class most days. She always tries to help all the kids, not just the ones who get services. She's worked with Red ever since pre-K. But for the last two weeks, Ms. Yvonne hasn't been here. Well, she's been here, but not in Room 208. She's had to give the makeup tests to the kids in other grades who missed their standardized tests last month.

"So tell us about this T-word already," Avery said.

"Next Wednesday is going to be a long day," Mr. Acevedo said. He tucked some hair behind his ears. "There's a morning section and an afternoon section."

"It's all writing?" Olivia asked.

"We think so," Ms. Yvonne said.

"Think?" a few kids said at once.

"It's a language arts test," Mr. Acevedo said. "That's pretty much all we know."

"Didn't the teachers have to go to a meeting about it yesterday?" Xander asked.

"We did," Ms. Yvonne said. "They kept us here until six-thirty going over the procedures."

"That must've been fun," Avery said, rolling her neck.

"No comment," Mr. Acevedo said.

"Are we done yet?" Attie asked. She waved her purple folder with the word *GRADUATION* written in all caps across the front. "I want to talk about Gala25."

"We're almost done," Mr. Acevedo said.

Attie is the student representative on the graduation festivities committee. For the last few weeks, she's been giving regular updates during CC.

I stared at the water bottle by her feet. It was the party favor from her brother's bar mitzvah last year. Everyone got one. I still had mine.

Attie had to know about Hoops Machine, but she wasn't going to say anything, was she? Mr. Acevedo said they were trying to keep the performance under wraps. Did Attie know I knew? Did she know I was playing?

"What if we don't want to take the T-word?" Avery asked.

Her question jolted me out of my mind wander.

"Excuse me?" Mr. Acevedo said.

"What if we don't want to take it?" Avery squeezed her brakes. "What if we refuse?"

"I'm not sure how that would work," he said.

"Yo, it is messed up we have to take a T-word two days before graduation," Diego said.

"It's friggin' ridiculous," Avery said. She rolled forward and quarter-turned so she faced everyone. "Haven't we taken enough tests already? You really think this test is going to make a difference?"

"Can we not do this now?" Attie said, standing up. "We're supposed to be talking about Gala25."

"You really think they're ever going to tell us the results?" Avery continued. "They're not going to finish grading it until next year. This test is pointless." She faced Mr. Acevedo again. "Why do we have to take it?"

"Why?" Mr. Acevedo grabbed his ankles and recrossed his legs.

"Yeah, why?" Avery said. "What would—"

"Seriously, stop," Attie said. "The fifth grade gets to have a separate party room away from the grown-ups." She pulled a sheet from her folder. "DJ Smitty is spinning. There's going to be a costume photo booth. It's going to be so dope. That's what we should be talking about right now."

"No," Avery said. "I want to know why we have to take this T-word."

"Because we're lab rats!" Attie said.

"Lab rats?" Red made a face.

"Like we're rats in a lab," Attie said. "Like, for experiments."

"Lab rats," Red said, nodding. "Got it. Thanks, Attie Silverman."

"Hold on," Mr. Acevedo said, motioning to Attie. "I need to jump in here. Lab rats? I don't think that's entirely accurate."

"Yes, it is," Attie said. "We're like lab rats having to take all these T-words." She swatted her folder against the couch's armrest.

"Well, your definition of a lab rat is accurate," Mr. Acevedo said, "but I don't think it applies to this situation. If this were a field T-word next Wednesday, I'd be inclined to agree. But this is a real T-word."

I had learned all about field tests from Mom. Field tests are when the big testing companies make fake tests and then try them out on kids. They're supposed to help the testing companies create the real tests.

Mom refused to make the kids at her school take them. She sent them back to the testing company unopened, and in her cover letter, she let them know her students weren't "lab rats" for their product development. Mom took serious heat from her district for it, but the parents at her school loved that she stood up for the kids. Mom thinks it's why when it came time for the real tests, all the kids took them.

"They can't make us take this T-word," Avery said.

"No one can make you do anything," Mr. Acevedo said.

"What if a bunch of us refused?" Avery said. "What if we all refused?" She rolled her neck. "What could they do to us?"

Bubba and Buggin'

"Be right back!" Red said, swinging the poop bag.

"Thanks for picking that up," I said.

"Of course, Mason Irving," he said as he raced off.

I pointed at Bubba sitting in the middle of the yard. "Stay, girl."

I was on the steps of our back deck with my journal in my lap. I'd brought it outside because I thought I'd finally write in it, but instead, I ended up watching Red and Bubba.

From around the side of the house, I heard Red lift the metal lid of the poop pail and then, a second later, close it back up. Bubba's ears rose and curled with the sounds.

"Stay," I said again. "Good girl."

I still hadn't told Red about Hoops Machine. And I hadn't spoken to him about his episode in class. I wanted to ask him about that first, but I needed to wait for the right moment, and so far, the right moment hadn't arrived.

I glanced over my shoulder at the kitchen window. In a

few minutes, Mom would call us in. Red was eating over, and like every weeknight when he had dinner here, Mom was making barbecue chicken, salad (with extra cucumbers and no tomatoes), and chips with guacamole.

"Did you miss me, Bubba Chuck?" Red asked, bolting back into the yard.

You know those videos of soldiers returning home from a tour in the military, the ones when they're first reunited with their dog and the dog goes absolutely bonkers? Well, Bubba acts like one of those dogs every time she sees Red. He'll be gone for five seconds—like right now—and she'll act like he's been gone a year!

"Did you miss me, Bubba Chuck?" He baseball-slid onto the grass. "Did you?"

Bubba climbed onto his chest and licked his face.

"Did you, Bubba Chuck?" Red giggled as he tried to dodge her tongue. "Did you?"

"She misses you when she blinks," I said. I stood up and tossed my journal onto the deck. "Hey, what happened in class yesterday?"

"What happened in class yesterday?" Red asked, blocking Bubba's tongue with his hand.

"You know," I said. "When you . . . when you stood up and started to bug."

"Oh," Red said. He made a face. "I was excited. Then the chair fell over and everyone . . . everyone was laughing.

I was embarrassed. Everyone was . . . everyone was looking at me because . . . I was excited because Mr. Acevedo drew a perfect circle with his finger, but . . ." He shrugged. "I was excited and . . . I got embarrassed."

"That's it?" I asked.

"That's it, Mason Irving."

I knew it was. Red's not exactly the lying type.

With my eyes, I traced a path to Red and Bubba. Then I rocked in place, shook out my arms, and took off.

I did a full flip and stuck the landing.

"Boo-yah!" I hammer-fisted the air.

"Sick!" Red said. "When did you learn to do that?"

"I've been teaching myself," I said. I dove next to Red and rolled onto my back. Bubba bounded right over. "You're getting so big, girl!" I said, picking her up.

A few weeks ago, I could hold her up forever, but now I needed to put her down after a few seconds.

"This is why we always pick up your poop," I said, rolling on the grass with her. "If we didn't, we'd be rolling on land mines."

"I'm definitely not rolling on land mines," Red said. He sat up. "I'm not picking up carrot poops, either."

"Carrot poops! Ha!"

Baby carrots are Bubba's favorite treats, but Red and I learned the hard way what happens when you give her too many. Picking up those orange, runny, stinky . . . Well, you get the picture.

Ever since the orange-poop incident, Red won't go near one of Bubba's poops if there's any orange in it at all. To be perfectly honest, I can't really complain—my best friend picks up my dog's poops! He changes her pee pads, too, which is awesome because Bubba is a peeing machine, which if you think about it makes total sense because her puppy bladder is the size of a Ping-Pong ball, and after she drinks even a few slurps of water, that liquid has to go somewhere!

"So I got some news," I said, sitting up. I put Bubba next to me.

"What kind of news?"

"Good news," I said. "Great news."

"What kind of great news?" Red bounced.

"You're going to bug," I said, smiling. "But not bug like you did in class yesterday."

Red made a face. "Very funny, Mason Irving."

Up until this year, I would've never teased Red like that. He wouldn't have known I was joking, and there's a good chance he would've bugged out.

"You can't tell anyone," I said. I crossed my legs and grabbed my ankles.

"That's how Mr. Acevedo sits," Red said, pointing. "You're sitting like Mr. Acevedo."

"I mean it, Red," I said. "It's a secret. You can't tell anyone."

He tapped his legs, pinky-thumb-pinky-thumb-pinky-thumb, which meant he was concentrating.

"It's about Gala25," I said. "I know the big surprise guest."

"Who's the big surprise guest?" He bounced faster.

"Hoops Machine."

"Hoops Machine?" Red grabbed his head. "Hoops Machine?"

I grinned. "Hoops Machine."

"I love Hoops Machine!" Red popped to his feet and raised his fists. "That's the greatest news in the history of ever."

I stood, too. "No, it's not," I said.

Red lowered his hands. "It's not?"

"Nope," I said. "This is." I tapped my chest. "I'm playing with Hoops Machine."

"What?" His fists shot back up. "Wow, wow, wow!"

Suddenly, Red hugged me. Red *never* hugged me first. We hug from time to time—which is amazing because up until not that long ago, Red couldn't stand it when anyone touched him—but Red never started our hugs. I always did.

"How sick is that, Red!" I said, leaping into the air and punching the sky. "It's the sickest news in the history of ever."

"The sickest news in the history of ever!"

Bubba stood on her hind legs and put her paws on me.

"Down, Bubba," I said. I grabbed her paws and shook them back and forth. "Down, girl."

"Tell her 'Off,'" Red said. "Hold up your hands and say 'Off.'"

"Off." I lowered her to the grass and held up my hands. She jumped on Red.

"Off, Bubba Chuck," Red said firmly. He held up his hands. "Off."

She got down right away.

"The Dog Whisperer returns," I said.

"I speak the language of puppies," Red said.

"You do."

"Stay, Bubba Chuck." Red pointed at her and looked at me. "When you tell Bubba Chuck to do something, you have to mean it. You can't tell Bubba Chuck to get off and hold her paws at the same time. Bubba Chuck will never learn. Dogs think differently than humans."

"My bad," I said.

"Dogs always need to know you're the one in control," Red said. "Dogs always need to know you're the boss."

"Boss!" I thumped my chest.

"Hoops Machine is boss," Red said, hopping from foot to foot. "Groll is my favorite player on Hoops Machine. Groll's dunks are sick. Then Rekate. Rekate is my second-favorite player on Hoops Machine. The way Rekate dribbles when she's sitting is nuts. Then Ruiz. Ruiz is my third-favorite player on Hoops Machine."

Yeah, Red can name all the players on Hoops Machine.

"I'm in basketball mode," I said, pretending to take a shot. "Full-throttle basketball mode."

"Full-throttle basketball mode," Red said. "I like that."

"You should have seen me out there, Red. I killed it."

"What?" Red grabbed his head again. "You played with Hoops Machine?"

"I had my first practice yesterday."

"Yesterday?" Red hopped faster. "Why didn't you say anything?"

"I only found out yesterday."

"Oh, man!" Red basketball-smiled and shook his fists next to his ears. "You played with Groll? You played with Rekate? You played with Ruiz?"

"I played with all of them," I said. "Groll, Rekate, Ruiz, Croft. You should see Croft do his moves in person. It's next level."

"Next level!"

"I told them about you," I said.

"Me?" Red pointed to himself. "You told Hoops Machine about me?"

"I told them you were a beast from the line."

"You did? What did Hoops Machine say? What did Hoops Machine say, Mason Irving?"

I shrugged. "They didn't really care," I said, smiling.

Red made a face. "Very funny, Mason Irving."

"Ha!" I bumped his shoulder. "Hoops Machine gave me a nickname. Ruiz gave it to me."

"Ruiz gave you a nickname? What's the nickname?"

"You ready?" I said. "Hoops Skywalker!"

"Hoops Skywalker!" Red started hopping again. "Wow, wow, wow!" He held out his shaking hands. "You need to stop, Mason Irving. I don't know how much more great basketball news I can take."

"Ha!" I said. "Mega-Man was there."

"Mega-Man?" Red froze.

Yesterday at practice, the moment Ruiz said Mega-Man's name, my brain shot to Mega-Man's father. I stared at Red. That's exactly what had just happened to him. That's what must happen to everyone these days. I wondered if Mega-Man knew. He had to.

"Mega-Man's playing also," I said.

"Mega-Man's father had a heart attack." Red raised his knuckles to his cheeks.

"I know," I said.

"Did Mega-Man . . . Did Mega-Man say anything about his father?"

"No," I said.

"Did you ask Mega-Man about his father?"

I shook my head. "Mega-Man's performing with the HM Flyers," I said. "He gets to dunk." I picked up Bubba's Frisbee. "Come here, girl," I said.

Bubba scooted over.

"Sit," I said, raising my open hand. Bubba sat. "Good girl." I scratched under her chin.

Then Bubba and I played tug-of-war with the Frisbee. I pulled and shook it hard, but no matter how hard I did, Bubba didn't let go. A few times, I even lifted her off the ground.

"Release, Bubba," I said firmly. "Release."

Bubba loosened her jaws and opened her mouth.

"Good girl." I scratched under her chin again.

"Can I show you something?" Red said, calling for the Frisbee.

I tossed it to him.

"Watch this," he said.

Red began playing catch with Bubba. With each throw, you could almost see her getting better and better.

"Great catch, Bubba Chuck!" Red said when Bubba made a leaping, twisting grab.

Bubba puppy-galloped back to Red and dropped the Frisbee into his palm.

"Now watch this, Mason Irving." Red waved the Frisbee. "You ready, Bubba Chuck? You ready?"

Red threw the Frisbee into the yard. Bubba turned and gave chase. She picked it up and brought it back. Red threw it a second time. Bubba turned and gave chase again.

"What am I watching?" I asked.

Red grinned. "Bubba Chuck is like Derek Zoolander."

"Zoolander?" I said. "Like the movie?"

Red and I had watched *Zoolander* over Easter break. We love every movie with Will Ferrell. We've seen *Elf* and *Talladega Nights* a gazillion times. Okay, maybe not a gazillion, but we've seen them a lot.

"Derek Zoolander can't turn left," Red said, laughing. "Bubba Chuck can't turn left."

He waved the Frisbee above her snoot and then threw it over her head to the left. When Bubba turned to give chase, she spun right and circled back left.

"See!" Red laughed harder. "Bubba Chuck isn't an ambi-turner!"

"Ambi-turner!" I clapped. "That's amazing! How did you notice that?"

" 'I'm not an ambi-turner,' " Red said, reciting the movie line and imitating Zoolander. " 'It's a problem I had since I was a baby. I can't turn left.' "

"Bubba can't go left," I said.

"Derek Zoolander can't go left," Red said. "Bubba Chuck can't go left. Mason Irving can't go left."

I bumped Red's shoulder. "I can go left."

"Not as well as you can go right."

"I'm playing with Hoops Machine these next two weeks," I said, "and I'm playing ball every single day this summer. By the time I set foot on the court for middle school tryouts, you won't be able to tell if I'm a righty or a lefty!"

The Book Stairs Boycott

The next day, instead of heading out to recess after lunch, I stayed in the cafeteria with Diego, Attie, and Avery. To be perfectly honest, I wanted to be outside playing *American Ninja Warrior* on the playground, but Avery had insisted that I stay behind to talk about the test. I told her I would if she convinced Attie to stay, too.

I underestimated Avery's powers of persuasion.

"Dude, you know this is a good idea," Avery said to Attie.

"No, I don't," Attie said.

"You wouldn't be here if you didn't."

"Yo, I'm down for a boycott," Diego said. "They're not going to do anything to us if we don't take it."

"I wouldn't be so sure." Attie squeezed her water bottle.

"They won't do a thing." Diego waved his spork. "They didn't make us build the community garden."

Last fall, when we got busted for Operation Food Fight,

our "punishment" was to build a community garden, but we never had to. Everything was in place and ready to go, but then the district changed its mind about the location and never got around to approving another spot.

"I'll bet you anything it's one of those tests where we're not expected to know all the answers," Avery said.

"It'd better not be," Attie said.

"Dude, I'll bet you anything it is," Avery said.

"Those tests make no sense." Attie squeezed her water bottle again. "Why test us on something we're not supposed to know?"

"Why should we take it?" Avery said. "That's the better question."

My mind revved listening to Diego, Attie, and Avery. I heard Mom's words from the other day about last-minute surprises:

Far too often, someone does something I really wish they hadn't, and then I have to spend way too much time cleaning up the mess.

I pressed my thumbs and knuckles to my lips. Mom would freak if she knew about this. Freak. But I wasn't a part of this. I was just sitting in the cafeteria, listening to my friends' conversation. I hadn't said a word. There was no *this*.

My brain bounced to what Ruiz had told me at the end

of practice Monday. About trusting my instincts and following my heart. About knowing what's right and knowing who I was. About being true. It was almost as if she was talking about *this*.

"Yo, we're going rogue!" Diego said, banging the table. "Going rogue and boycotting the test."

"Calm down, dude," Avery said.

"It would be pretty dope," Attie said.

"It would be sick!" Diego banged the table again. "Going rogue and—"

"There you are!"

We all turned. Red was speed-walking our way across the cafeteria. Melissa, Noah, and Olivia were right behind him.

"Why didn't you come outside?" Red asked.

"We're trying to figure something out," Attie answered.

Red spun his headphones around his wrist. "What are you trying to figure out, Attie Silverman?"

"Next week's test," Diego said. "We're going rogue."

"Going rogue?" Red made a face.

My basketball eyes checked the door. Ms. Dunwoody and her first graders were lined up for the next lunch period.

"Let's talk not talk about this here," I said, standing up. "I know where to go."

* * *

As we headed out of the cafeteria, my brain revved even faster, jumping from thought to thought to thought.

I stared at the headphones Red was still spinning around his wrist. Red loves spinning and twirling things—napkins, coins, pens, plates, you name it. He's able to do some pretty cool tricks, too, especially with his headphones. Red used to take earplugs or noise-canceling headphones everywhere because he hated loud noises. He still doesn't like them, but for the most part, he no longer needs the headphones or earplugs.

My mind hopped to Avery. I'd known she was serious about not taking the test, but I hadn't realized how serious. Now Diego was with her, and she was on her way to convincing Attie, if she hadn't already. I definitely needed to stop underestimating Avery's powers of persuasion.

I thought about Mom. Before testing last month, a few RJE parents had asked her about refusing the tests. But after what happened with the field tests at her school, she wouldn't get involved. She wanted no part of it.

It's a personal decision each family has to make with his or her own child.

That was her line. I'd heard her say it a gazillion times. Okay, maybe not a gazillion, but she said it a lot.

Yeah, Mom would freak if she knew about this.

* * *

The Book Stairs is what the K-1 staircase is now called. Earlier in the year, a group of kindergarten parents painted the fronts of each step so that they looked like the spines of books. Each grade got to vote for two books. We chose *Bud, Not Buddy* and *Rules*.

Since the first graders were at lunch and the kindergartners never went to the second floor in the afternoon, I knew we'd have the Book Stairs to ourselves. We all walked there together, except for Avery. Avery took the elevator so she could sit on the second-floor landing.

"I heard Ms. Hamburger's coming to Gala25," Olivia said.

"She is?" Melissa and Noah said at the same time.

Attie nodded. "She's supposed to."

"Sweet!" Diego said.

"The Lunch Bunch is coming, too," Olivia said.

"Why are we talking about Gala25?" Avery snarled.

"Ms. Eunice, Ms. Carmen, Ms. Joan, Ms. Audrey, and Ms. Liz are coming to Gala25?" Red said. He held his headphones, which were now around his neck.

"They all are," Olivia said.

The Lunch Bunch were the lunch ladies who used to work at RJE. Everyone had loved them, but this year, because of all the crazy budget cuts, the district hired a different food service that wasn't nearly as friendly.

roy and Toa

ad Kitty

Frindle

Buddy

Rules

OTIS

I HEAR A PICKLE

The Hobbit

"I'm telling you," Attie said, "Gala25 is going to be so dope. Ms. Hamburger is coming, the Lunch Bunch is coming, the—"

"Enough with the Gala25 chitchat," Avery interrupted.

"How can you be so sure the Lunch Bunch is coming back?" Noah said. "They didn't come back for School Lunch Hero Day."

"Yo, the Lunch Bunch didn't come back for School Lunch Hero Day because Principal Darling canceled School Lunch Hero Day," Diego said.

"That's not what happened," I said. "The new lunch ladies didn't—"

"Stop!" Avery pounded her armrest. "I swear, the next person who says a friggin' word about Gala25 or the Lunch Bunch is getting run over."

"Tell us how you really feel, Avery?" I said, smiling.

Everyone laughed.

She flung a pencil at me. It sailed over my head.

"Calm down," I said, still smiling.

"Dude, this is calm," Avery said. "You'll know when I'm not calm. We're supposed to be talking about the test."

"The test!" Diego popped to his feet and charged up the steps. "We're going rogue!"

"You really like that word, don't you?" I said.

"I do." Diego bounced like he had springs in his sneakers. "Rogue, rogue, rogue."

"Don't play!" Avery rammed him with her chair.

"Yo!" Diego backed into the wall. "No need to get violent."

"I'm boycotting the test," she said. "I don't care about the rest of you."

"Yes, you do, Avery Goodman," Red said, still gripping his headphones. "You do care. That's why you're here."

"Ha!" I pointed at Avery. "Truth!"

"We all care," Red said. "That's why we're all here."

"Whatever, dude," Avery said.

"Yo, even though you just attacked me," Diego said to Avery, "I'm still with you. Count me in."

"Count me in, too," Attie said. She had her elbows on her knees and held her hands with the tips of her fingers touching. "Making us take a test the third-to-last day of school is plain wrong."

"If you think about it," Avery said, rolling to the edge of the step, "we're doing exactly what Mr. Acevedo has been telling us to do all year. We're expressing ourselves."

"We celebrate our voices in Room 208," Diego said, imitating Mr. Acevedo. He pulled back his hair and pretended to adjust an earring. "How can we make our voices heard beyond these four walls? How can we amplify our voices?"

Everyone laughed.

Except for me.

"We need more kids," I said, standing up.

"Word," Attie said. "If we're really doing this, we need more kids."

"We need friggin' everyone," Avery said.

"Or as close to everyone as we can get," I said, leaning against the railing on the *Frindle* step. "Strength in numbers."

"We're going rogue!" Diego jumped in a circle.

"Everyone, try to get more kids," Attie said. "We'll meet again at lunch tomorrow."

"Friday," I said. "That gives us a little more time."

"Friday it is," Attie said.

"Do we tell our parents?" Noah asked.

"No!" Attie and Avery said at the same time.

My eyes shot to Red. He was still gripping his headphones, and now he was hunching his shoulders and bouncing his knees, too.

"But they're going to find out," Noah said. "Once we—"

"Dude, no," Avery said, cutting him off. "Yeah, they're going to find out, but we don't need to be the ones to tell them."

"When you talk to other kids," Attie said, "tell them not to say anything to their parents."

I pressed my fist to my chin and closed my eyes. I wasn't going to say anything to Mom, but she was going to find out, and she wasn't going to like it.

Not. At. All.

"The other day," I said, brushing the locks off my forehead, "Mr. Acevedo told me a new word equation."

"Yo, is this going to be corny?" Diego said.

"Oh, yeah!" Red laughed. "This is definitely going to be corny."

"You're corny at school," Diego said. "You're corny at hoops. You're just mad corny, Rip."

"Mad corny," I said, smiling. I walked along the *Bad Kitty* step. "Mr. Acevedo told me the next word equation. It's the last one of the year."

Avery rolled her eyes. "This is going to be so friggin' corny," she said.

"Luck equals preparation plus opportunity," I said. "We make our own luck, and luck happens when preparation and opportunity come together." I brought my fists together and knocked the knuckles. "It's time to make some luck."

Strength in Numbers

On Friday, we couldn't hold the lunchtime boycott meeting on the Book Stairs because twice as many kids showed up. So we moved the meeting to the walkway that leads into the playground. Or, I should say, Attie moved it. She was all business, in charge and on point.

"We're up to sixteen kids," Attie said, once everyone had gathered. "This is so dope."

"Strength in numbers!" Red said, raising his fist.

I held up mine. He gave me a pound.

Red sat beside me on the bench closest to the playground. His other hand rested on one of *our* posts. The summer before third grade, when the whole community pitched in to build the playground, Red and I helped put in the wooden posts with the solar lights that lined the walkway.

"We still need more kids," Avery said. She sat on the bench facing us, next to Attie. "We don't have enough."

"I'm with Avery," I said. "We still don't have enough kids."

"Who else can we get?" Attie asked.

"I'll talk to Miles and Sebi," Xander said.

"I'll say something to Gavin," Hunter said as he wheeled up and down the walkway in Avery's chair. "This is so much harder than it looks," he said to her. "How do you do it?"

"Really, dude?" Avery rolled her eyes. "I have a choice?"

I slid off the bench and sat down on the ground. "Anyone say anything to their parents?" I asked.

No one answered.

"Any grown-ups?" Attie added. "Anyone say anything to an older brother or sister?"

Nothing.

I kicked out my legs and began typewriter-dribbling my basketball. I wasn't buying the wall of silence. Someone had to have said something. Fifth graders aren't exactly known for secret-keeping abilities.

But then again, Mom didn't know. If anyone had told their parents, the parents would've e-mailed or called Mom in a heartbeat, and then Mom would've said something to me.

That's how things flow at RJE.

"What about Mr. Acevedo?" I asked. "Does he know?"

"He would've said something," Grace said.

"He knows something's up," Avery said. "No way he doesn't."

"I have a question about the test," Noah said, wiping his chin with his sleeve like always. "What do we do? Do we go to class or do we—"

"Yo, you bubble in the scan sheet," Diego said.

"Noah asked a good question," Attie said. "Not everyone knows that. When you get your test packet, the scan sheet has an opt-out bubble in the top right corner. Just fill it in. That means you're choosing not to take the test."

"We don't have to say anything?" X asked.

"No." Attie shook her head. "Mr. Acevedo will know what's up. You know he'll be cool. So will Ms. Yvonne."

"Oh, yeah," Red said. "Ms. Yvonne will definitely be cool."

Ms. Yvonne gave the tests to the kids who took them in separate locations.

"What happens after?" Noah asked.

"Principal Darling gets involved," X said. "And our parents."

"That's why it's important we all stick together," Attie said.

"Just like you said, Rip," Red said, raising both fists. "Strength in numbers!"

Bubba Time

"Check out this video," I said to Bubba.

I was on my bed, sitting cross-legged with my back against the wall and my laptop beside me. The computer

had been on my lap, but it had gotten too hot, and as soon as I moved it, Bubba put her head on my leg.

On the screen, the HM Flyers sprang off a mini trampoline and passed the basketball off the backboard. The last in line, Wicks, caught the ball with two hands and tomahawk-slammed it while doing a split.

"It's a gazillion times better in person," I said.

Ever since getting out of school yesterday, I'd been in full-throttle basketball mode—watching vids, practicing dribbling, working on my shooting, and watching more vids. The timer on my phone was counting down how long until the start of tomorrow morning's Hoops Machine practice.

Fourteen hours, thirty-six minutes, forty-one seconds.

"I'm playing with them, Bubba," I said. "How sick is that?" I leaned down and kissed the top of her head. "I still need to show you the vid where they're all doing the twisting somersault dunks. It's nuts!"

She shifted her head toward my drawstrings and opened her mouth.

"Don't even think it," I said.

Bubba has a thing for chewing on drawstrings. Earbuds and shoelaces, too. But she wasn't getting near my throwback Pistons shorts, the ones Dad got me before he went back to Asia for work.

"You have the softest ears, girl," I said, rubbing the tip of one with my thumb and finger. "Has anyone ever told you that?"

The next video began to play. Croft was performing his intro sequence—popping wheelies, starting and stopping, and changing direction, all while spinning a ball on his finger and rolling it across his chest and up and down his arms.

Just like I saw him do in person.

Ruiz was in the video, too. She was juggling three basketballs, mixing in under-the-leg and behind-the-back tosses. Of course, she was talking the whole time.

I heard her voice in my head:

Trust your instincts. Off the court as much as you do on the court. Follow that heart of yours. You know what's right.

I shook out my dreads and thought about the boycott. I was following my heart. I wasn't just going along with it because of my friends and classmates. Maybe I had been at first, but not anymore.

"Right, Bubba?" I said.

I adjusted the waistband of my shorts and saw where I'd written *Rip Hamilton* and *#32* in blue Sharpie along the inside of the elastic. I'd written it the day my dad gave me the shorts, the same day he told me about the real origin of my nickname.

I let out a puff. Bubba's head shot up. I'd blown right in her ear.

"Sorry, girl," I said, laughing. I lowered her head back to my leg. "It's okay."

I looked at the screen again. The next Croft vid had started playing. He was taking shots from the corner. I pictured Avery taking shots from the corner with Hoops Machine. She had to play with them, too.

I peeked down at Bubba. She was fighting to keep her half-open eyes from closing. I kissed the top of her head again.

She sighed with her whole body.

"Practice is going to be lit tomorrow."

HM Flyers

"You ready?" Croft called.

At the far end of the court, Wicks raised a fist.

Croft swivel-turned to Mega-Man. "Are you?"

"I'm ready," he said.

So was I.

I was standing along the baseline with the rest of Hoops Machine. Make that, the Hoops Machine crew were standing. I was jumping, shaking, and about to explode. Why? The HM Flyers were performing right in front of me!

Down the floor, Wicks and the four other Flyers—Arnold, Peskin, Bray, and Gersh—were lined up under the basket. At this end, Mega-Man was crouching beside Croft, parked just beyond the three-point circle.

"When I say 'set,'" Croft told Mega-Man, "you get in position." He pointed to the trampoline angled in place near the foul line. "When I say 'up,' you raise that ball."

Mega-Man wrapped his arms around the basketball and

held it against his Donald Duck T-shirt. "I'm ready," he said again.

"Here we go!" Croft announced.

Wicks sprinted for the trampoline. When he crossed midcourt, Arnold took off from the baseline, and Peskin got set to run. As Wicks leaped for the trampoline, Croft underhanded the ball off the backboard. Wicks sprang into the air, caught the ball overhead, and tossed it off the backboard like a soccer player on an inbounds throw. Arnold jumped next. He snared the basketball with two hands and spiked it.

"Set!" Croft called.

Mega-Man charged onto the court, holding his ball with both hands. He reached the side of the trampoline just as Peskin bounded off. She caught Arnold's spiked ball on the up-bounce and threw down a monster slam.

"Up!"

With one hand, Mega-Man raised his basketball and stood like the Statue of Liberty. Gersh flew off the trampoline, plucked the ball from Mega-Man, and front-flipped into a two-handed dunk.

"On fire!" Croft shouted. "That's how it's done!"

"Boo-yah!" I hammer-fisted the air and bolted to Mega-Man. "That was sick!" I held up both hands.

He double high-fived me hard. "I know!"

For less than a nanosecond, my brain flashed to Coach

Crazy. Coach Crazy had had a heart attack. I felt so awful for Mega-Man. I felt . . .

I bopped the side of my head and spun to Ruiz. "I want to dunk," I said.

"Man, this kid wants to be the whole show!" Groll said.

"Check out my ups." I hopped onto the trampoline.

"Hoops Skywalker," Ruiz said, waving me back. "We here. We going over the show deets." She pounded a basketball. "The gym on Saturday has up-to-date electrical. We gots full sound and lights. So we bringing the new strobes. We finally getting to work the new lighting into the program."

I raised my hand. Ruiz nodded to me.

"My friend Red?" I said. "The one I told you about who makes the underhanded free throws?" I pretended to shoot one. "He gets freaked out by strobe lights."

"So does my son," Ruiz said.

"Red doesn't like loud noises, either," I said, "but he can deal with them. The strobe lights—"

"We hold off on the strobes for another week," Ruiz said, cutting me off. "Mad props, mad props for looking out for your boy."

"Thanks," I said. "Can I tell you about my other friend?"

"Man, this kid is something else," Groll said.

"Her name's Avery," I said. "Avery Goodman. She just started playing wheelchair basketball. It'd be unbelievable if she could play with Hoops Machine because she—"

"We'll get her out there," Groll said.

I heel-turned to him. "You will?"

"We will," Sinanis said. "As principal, it is so ordered!"

Everyone laughed. Except Mega-Man and me.

Sinanis stepped to us. "Sinanis isn't my real name," he said, smiling.

"It's not?" Mega-Man said.

"Nope," he replied. "It's a nickname. A couple years ago at a school show, I borrowed the principal's ID for one of the bits, but I forgot to give it back. When I e-mailed Principal Sinanis the next day to tell him, he told me to keep the ID as a souvenir. So I did. But then I made the mistake of trying it on without knowing these guys over here happened to be watching." He thumbed his teammates. "I had it on for less than five seconds, but that's all it took. A nickname was born. Sinanis."

I shook out my dreads and pinched my forearm. I was standing on a basketball court and hanging out with Hoops Machine! My Hoops Machine fantasy was really happening.

"Tell them about your name," Croft said to Groll.

"I was waiting for one of you clowns to go there," Groll said.

"What's up with your name?" I asked.

Groll wagged a finger at me. "This kid is something else."

"We like this kid a lot," Skeggs said, mocking Groll. "Man, this kid is something else. When Groll first joined the team, he spent all his time on his screens watching the news."

"But he wasn't interested in the news," Croft said. "He had a crush on this one reporter. We all busted him."

Mega-Man and I laughed.

Croft scooped up the ball by Sinanis's feet. "Do you know what the reporter's name was?" he said as he wheeled off.

"What?" Mega-Man asked.

"Groll!" I shouted.

"You got it!" Skeggs said. "Now, to be fair, reporter Groll was adorable. Those blue eyes of his were to die for."

My basketball eyes spotted Croft dribbling at fast-break speed toward a side hoop. Groll sprinted after him.

"You think you're getting past me?" Groll said, cutting off his lane.

"I know I am," Croft said.

In wheelchair basketball, you can pick up your dribble and start dribbling again. That's not considered traveling. But you're not allowed to push more than twice without dribbling. That is traveling.

Right now, Croft was putting on a basketball-skills dance—starting and stopping, rolling and dribbling, flipping the ball around his back and over his lap. He had Groll tripping over his feet.

"Careful there," Croft said. "You might break those ankles."

"Man, you're dreaming if you think you're getting past me." Groll swiped at the ball and elbowed Croft's backrest.

Croft put the ball in his lap, pushed forward once, and then with one arm, shoved Groll away and cleared enough space to get off a shot.

Swish.

"I'm your nightmare!" Croft pointed at him with his index fingers. "I own you." He spun around and headed back to us.

"Okay, then," Ruiz said. "Saturday's show. We focus, we focus."

"I want to dunk," I said, stepping forward.

"We heard you the first time," Bailey said.

"Just once." I looked at Ruiz. "Let me throw one down."

"Kid, you are a piece of work," Groll said.

"The run-up-the-players'-backs dunk," I said. "Let me do it once."

"Right now, right now?" Ruiz said.

I shook out my dreads. "Right now, right now."

* * *

One at a time, I lifted my legs and pulled my socks all the way up. Then I took the ball off the rack and gazed downcourt. In the paint at the far end, Bray, Wicks, Gersh, Peskin, and Arnold were lined up in size order, bent over, and holding on to each other's legs. The trampoline was positioned inside the top of the key, tilted toward the basket.

I squeezed the basketball. I was about to do the HM Flyers running dunk.

"You ready?" Croft called.

I raised my fist.

"Let's see what you got, Jedi," he said.

I bolted from the baseline.

Past the foul line.

Past midcourt.

Full speed.

At the trampoline, I kept on running and sprang forward, charging up the backs of Bray, Wicks, and Gersh. Then I ran onto Peskin, who was standing on the front of a second trampoline, and then onto Arnold, who stood on the other end of that trampoline supported by Sinanis.

I soared for the hoop.

"Boo-yah!"

A Perfectly
Executed Ambush

"I got to dunk! I got to dunk!" I leaped into the front seat
and flung my bag into the back. "They let me dunk, Mom!"
I kissed her on the cheek. "They let me dunk."

"Someone's excited," she said.

"They let me do the dunk where you run up the players'
backs." I hammer-fisted the air. "It was nuts!"

"Sorry I was a little late. The traffic on the—"

"You should've seen me throw it down." I bounced in
the seat. "I threw it down with authority. With authority!"

"Honey." She grabbed my knee and squeezed. "Relax.
Calm down a little."

"You should've seen Mega-Man." I gripped the door's
armrest. "He held the ball for the Statue of Liberty dunk."

I waited for her to ask what the Statue of Liberty dunk
was, but she didn't.

Whenever I tell Mom about my practices, I always go on
and on and on. And Mom always listens. Always. She even
asks questions. When my friends talk to their moms about

basketball or soccer or whatever, you can tell their moms aren't really listening.

Mom tapped the wheel with her fingernail and stared at the red light.

"When I got to practice," I said, bouncing again, "we rehearsed the introduction. They pretended to pull me onto the court and then Skeggs bounced a ball off the back of my head, and Bailey dribbled a ball off my butt, and Ruiz trash-talked me like nobody's business. Nobody's business! And then Groll elbowed me and called me Yoda, and that's when I told him I was Hoops Skywalker and stole the ball from him. Then I did my opening number. You should've seen me, Mom. I was lit! Then Croft went into this bit where he was one-wheel spinning, starting and stopping, and then the Flyers—"

I stopped.

"Earth to Mom," I said, rocking. "Come in, Mom."

"What?" she said. "I'm listening."

"No, you're not," I said. "You haven't heard a word I've said."

"Yes, I have," she said. "You're telling me about the opening. They pulled you onto the court and—"

"Nice try," I said. "So what is it?"

Her fingernails still tapped the wheel. She said nothing.

"What?" I said. "What did I do?"

She picked up her Perky's thermos from the console. "I spoke to Mr. Acevedo on the way here."

I stopped rocking.

This was bad. No, this was beyond bad. This was a perfectly executed Lesley Irving ambush. I was trapped in a long car ride home with no means of escape.

"I had a feeling he'd call you," I said.

"A feeling?"

"He told you about the—"

"Yes, he told me about your boycott, but you neglected to tell *me*," she said, raising her voice. "Why?"

I shrugged. "You were going to find out anyway."

"That's your answer?"

Mom wasn't just angry. She was in full principal mode. The last time she'd been in full principal mode with me was when we got busted for Operation Food Fight. Back in the fall, a few of us got caught shooting vids of the disgusting lunches being served in the cafeteria.

She sipped her coffee and placed the thermos back in the cup holder. "Were you ever planning on telling me about it?" she asked.

"Yeah," I said.

"Yeah?"

"Yes," I said. "I thought you'd be proud of me. You hate testing more than—"

"Stop," she said. "That's not what you thought here, Rip. You intentionally chose not to tell me."

I kicked off my sneakers and raised my knees.

"So when were you planning on telling me about all this?" she asked.

"Not until after," I said.

"Why not until after?" She clicked on the turn signal, checked the mirror, and changed lanes.

"We wanted to do it on our own," I said. "We didn't want to involve parents."

"You didn't want to involve parents? What did you think was going to happen, Rip?"

"It's not about you, Mom," I muttered.

"What?" She shot me a sideways glare.

"It's not about you," I said again.

"What's that supposed to mean?"

I let out a puff.

"Don't you sigh at me," she said through her teeth. "Start talking, Rip."

One by one, I pulled off my socks. Then I raised my knees again and wrapped my arms around my legs.

"I said, talk."

"It wasn't my idea," I said.

"You sure are going along with it."

"It was Avery's idea," I said. "She's the one who started it."

I had to tell Mom everything. It was in my best interest.
It was also in my best interest not to leave out any details. I
know how Mom is when she's like this.

"On Tuesday at CC, Avery started talking about how she
didn't want to take the test," I said. "She asked Mr. Acevedo
what would happen if she didn't. Then Attie got all heated
because we weren't talking about graduation stuff."

"How'd you get involved?"

"A bunch of us met and—"

"Who's a bunch?"

"Me, Avery, Attie, and Diego. We met at lunch the next day. Then Melissa, Olivia, Noah, and Red joined us."

Mom pursed her lips and shook her head. "I love how you involved Red in all this."

"I didn't involve Red. He involved himself."

"You know how he is, Rip."

"I do, Mom, but you don't."

"We're not making this about Red."

"He can make decisions for himself," I said. "You grown-ups need to let him."

"I said, we're not making this about Red."

I tell Mom all the time how grown-ups don't know Red like I do. They think they do, but they don't.

We merged onto the highway.

"Tell me about this meeting you and your classmates had."

"It was on the Book Stairs," I said. I put my legs back down. "Avery and Attie led it."

"I thought you said Attie was angry because Avery was talking about the test."

"She was, but the . . . the meeting was mostly about how this was our chance to stand up for ourselves. That's what

Mr. Acevedo's been telling us all year. He's always telling us our voices count and that what we have to say matters." I half smiled. "Then Diego started joking about how we were all going rogue."

"Lovely."

"We met again on Friday at recess," I said. "At the first meeting, we said we needed more kids. At the second meeting, more than half the class showed up." I flipped down the visor. "Strength in numbers."

Mom reached over and flipped it back up. "Strength in numbers?"

"If everyone was involved and we all stuck together, they couldn't do anything to us."

"Really? That's what you all thought?"

"They didn't do anything for Operation Food Fight."

"Are you kidding? You're using that as a precedent?"

I knew Operation Food Fight was a bad example. I'd known it was a bad example when Diego brought it up the other day, but I didn't say anything then.

"For smart kids," Mom said, "you really didn't think this one all the way through." She thumped the steering wheel with the heel of her hand. "When I heard about all this on Friday, I was—"

"You've known since Friday?" I said. "You waited until now to say something?"

"Oh, please, Rip," she said. "Don't you even think of trying to put this one on me. You did this."

I gripped the back of my neck. "You could've told me sooner."

"I could've told you sooner? I think you may have that backward."

"I can't believe you dropped a Sunday Night Bomb on me the last week of school."

"Honey, that's not what this is, and you know it."

A Sunday Night Bomb is when you wait until Sunday night to drop news you could've shared at any other time over the weekend. Like when you wait until eight o'clock on the Sunday night at the end of Christmas break to announce you have to interview your mom about her favorite holiday memory for the video you need for tomorrow.

I'm the master of Sunday Night Bombs.

"Who else knows about the boycott?" I asked.

"Who else knows?" She motioned to her charging phone. "Who doesn't know?" She banged the gearshift and pointed. "It's my turn to talk now. You're going to listen, and you're going to listen good."

I didn't have much of a choice. Make that, I didn't have any choice. If I so much as even looked out my window, I was getting smacked on the back of my head.

"Let me break this down for you," she said. "Let me start

with my school. I believe in full transparency. Full transparency means I keep my parents informed."

"I know," I said.

"I don't think you do," she said. "Because if you did, we wouldn't be having this conversation. I believe in full transparency because I want my school community to know what's going on. It saves me a lot of work and heartache."

I was going to say *I know* again, but I thought better of it.

"The last thing I need is for my school to find out second- or thirdhand that my son is boycotting the test their children have to take," she said. "That means I need to get ahead of the story. That means I need to tell them. I need to explain why it's okay for you to boycott this test, but it's not okay for their children." She thumped the steering wheel again. "I also need to share this with my assistant superintendents. They can make life very unpleasant for me."

I folded my arms across my chest. "What I do at my school shouldn't matter at yours."

"But it does, Rip. This is the real world. It does. So now I have to deal with my school community and quite possibly contend with a testing boycott situation I thought I'd avoided this year. But that's only the beginning. Now let's talk about your district, the one in which you're attending school for the next seven years."

I blinked hard and let out another puff.

"The parents may like me," she said, "but district leadership is a different story, and you know that. You know where I stand with that school board. I'm a thorn in their side, and they don't like that very much. Two of those board members outright despise me, but I couldn't care less because this is my son's education we're talking about, and they will be held accountable. But when my son gets involved in something like this . . ." She shook her head. "This is a bad time of year to poke the beast."

"What does that mean?"

She nodded to my window. "How am I on your side?"

I checked. "You can get over."

She clicked the turn signal and changed lanes again.

"Honey, you've seen the types of decisions the board has made," she said. "Their budget cuts, their last-century cell phone policy, the way they handled the hiring of the new lunch service, the way they're handling the influx of all these new students. Some of their decisions are absolutely asinine."

I knew what *asinine* meant. It meant foolish and ridiculous. Mom used the word a lot. Especially when it came to the school board.

"You've also seen the way they've responded to student incidents," she continued. "Just last month, that school board disbanded the middle school dance squad because they felt their uniforms were too revealing. I'm not looking forward to how they'll handle this situation, especially since they're up against a ticking clock." She picked up her thermos. "That's not working in your favor."

"Why not?"

"Rip, what did I say about last-minute surprises? This is the absolute worst time of year for something like this. The worst. If they handle this poorly—which is not unlikely—there isn't much time to make it right." She sipped her coffee and put it back in the cup holder. "I always tell you to pick your battles. I really wish you'd listened to me this time."

"I did listen."

"Then you and I have very different ideas about what the word *listen* means."

We got off the highway and stopped at the light at the end of the off ramp. We sat in silence, except for the sound of Mom's fingernails tapping on the steering wheel.

The light changed.

"I'm going to have to check in with Suzanne again when we get home," she said.

"She knows?"

"Of course she knows," Mom said. "This graduation means the world to her. She has such a wonderful surprise waiting for Red. If anything—"

"He's getting a dog, right?" I interrupted.

"Think about Suzanne," she said, ignoring my question. "Think about all she's been through. I have no idea how she's still upright after the hours she's been putting in. This graduation means . . ." Mom didn't finish the sentence.

To be perfectly honest, I hadn't thought much about Suzanne. It was kind of lame that I hadn't. I twisted a lock near my forehead at its root. The only times I had thought about her lately had to do with Red's dog. I couldn't wait for Red to get his dog. I couldn't wait for Bubba to have a friend.

"Do you think . . . Do you think they'd keep us from graduation?" I asked.

"They wouldn't dare," Mom said.

"What about . . . what about Gala25?"

"Gala25 has been a massive undertaking," she said. "If the district or the board starts playing games with it, there are going to be some very unhappy parents. Unfortunately, I wouldn't put it past them." She touched my leg with a finger. "You're going to be the most unhappy of all."

"Why me?"

"Why you? Has anything I've said during this car ride registered? If you don't take this test, you really think they're going to let you play with Hoops Machine?"

I flinched. "What?"

"Honey, I can assure you, there's no way they'll let you play."

"That's not fair!"

"Well, there's a simple—"

"That's so not fair, Mom!" I punched the door.

"Don't do that."

"It's not!"

"Like I said, I don't think you and your classmates thought this one all the way through."

"I have to play with Hoops Machine."

"I hate to tell you, Rip, but when it comes to my concerns, your playing with Hoops Machine is about here right now." She touched her shin with the side of her hand. "You sure misread the big-picture consequences on this one."

I could feel the tears filling in my eyes. "I have to play with Hoops Machine, Mom." I leaned forward and held my feet. "I have to."

"We play the cards we're dealt," she said. "I've told you that for as long as I can remember." She touched my leg again. "This time, you're the dealer who hasn't been paying attention. Time to get your head in the game before it's too late."

Elephants and Pickles

At the start of class the next morning . . .

"Welcome to the last full week of fifth grade!" Mr. Acevedo leaped into the air and kicked the heels of his high-
tops. "Our last Monday together."

"Here it comes again," Avery said, rolling her eyes. "All
sentimental all the time."

"All the time," Mr. Acevedo said. "If you thought I got
sentimental last week, just wait."

"We're still waiting for you to tell us your plans for next
year," Olivia said.

"You're going to have to wait a little longer for that," he
said.

"Still working on it, Mr. A.?" Xander asked, smiling.

"Still working on it, X." Mr. Acevedo strummed his
chest and then pointed to Red and Ms. Yvonne already sitting on the couch. "Let's all head on over to the meeting
area and start off our last week with CC."

Noah, Sebi, Hunter, and Declan dove for the beanbag chairs. Trinity and Ana climbed into the bathtub, and the OMG girls sat on the lip of it. Usually, only one person was allowed in the tub and only two people were allowed on the edge, but apparently, Mr. Acevedo was letting the rule slide this last week.

I sat on the floor in front of the couch and rubbed my eyes with my palms. I had barely slept at all the night before. I couldn't stop my brain from thinking about Hoops Machine. I still couldn't stop it. I had to play with Hoops Machine. This was my basketball fantasy. I couldn't miss out on this.

"These are Room 208 movie tickets," Mr. Acevedo said. He sat cross-legged in his usual spot on the rug and held up a stack of laminated cards. "You'll need a ticket to get into class tomorrow."

"We're going to the movies tomorrow?" Piper asked.

"Not exactly," Mr. Acevedo said. "We're doing an activity tomorrow."

"Are we watching a movie?" Sebi asked.

"Patience, grasshopper," Mr. Acevedo said. He handed the cards to Avery, sitting beside him. "Take one and pass the rest."

"Do we get a hint, Mr. A.?" Danny asked.

"A hint?" Mr. Acevedo tightened an earring. "It's going to be one of your favorite classes of the year."

"You call that a hint?" Miles said. "Can you—"

"Can we talk about the elephant in the room?" Attie said, cutting him off.

"There's an elephant in the room?" Red asked.

A few kids laughed.

"It's an expression," Ms. Yvonne said.

"It's what everyone is thinking about, but no one is talking about," Attie said. "The boycott."

The boycott.

A few times the night before, I had thought about backing out. I had. I'd be lying if I said I hadn't. But only for a little. I had to go along with it. And not just because everyone else was. Yeah, that was part of it, but this was something I *needed* to do.

"Here," Lana said, handing me the stack of cards.

I took mine and passed the rest on to Red.

"Yo, maybe there is an elephant in the room?" Diego said, bobbing his head and grinning. "Maybe Gerald's hiding in the closet."

"I love Elephant and Piggie," Sebi said. "I still have every book."

"I was Gerald for Halloween when I was little," Diego said.

"Dude, *when* you were little?" Avery said, rolling her neck. "I bet that costume still fits you."

Diego pretend-flexed. "Elephant and Piggie—"

"Enough with Elephant and Piggie," Avery said. "Can we talk about Wednesday?"

"We have strayed a little off topic." Mr. Acevedo recrossed his legs and motioned to Attie. "Let's talk about the elephant in the room. Let's talk about the boycott."

"We're doing it," Attie said.

"I know," Mr. Acevedo said. "Let's talk about it."

"You're not changing our minds," Avery said.

"Who says I want to?"

"Are you in trouble?" Noah asked.

"Me?" Mr. Acevedo pointed to himself. "Why would I be in trouble?"

"It's your class," Noah said.

"We've definitely gotten you in trouble, Mr. A.," Danny said.

"The superintendent's office has contacted me," Mr. Ace-vedo said.

"So you are in trouble," Noah said.

"What did you tell them?" Attie asked.

"I said there were kids in class who objected to taking a test such as this during the final week of school, and from what I understood, they were choosing not to take it."

Mr. Acevedo had a history of pushing the envelope this year. Back in the fall, he refused to do test prep in class, and even though he said he didn't get in trouble for that, we all know he did. Then when we got busted for Operation Food Fight, some of the district people thought he had something to do with it. Some of them still do.

They had to think he was involved with this. No doubt.

"Here's what I know," Mr. Acevedo said, tucking some hair behind his ears. "The powers that be are aware there's a testing rebellion brewing in Room 208."

"Yo, we've gone rogue!" Diego raised a fist.

"What does that mean for us?" Attie asked.

"It means you have their attention." Mr. Acevedo grabbed his ankles. "I'm pretty sure the district thought they'd made it through the year without having to deal with this issue."

"They thought wrong," Avery said.

My brain bounced back to the car ride with Mom

yesterday. She'd said almost the identical thing to me. She definitely talked about this with Mr. Acevedo.

"So this is a big deal," Olivia said.

"Yes," Mr. Acevedo said. "This is a big deal. The district knows their response will establish precedent, and if you don't know what precedent—"

"It means they're going to make an example of us," Attie said. "They don't want this to become a thing."

Mr. Acevedo held up the remaining movie tickets, which had made it back to him. "Everyone got one?" he asked.

Everyone had.

"We're all aware of the types of decisions this school board makes," Mr. Acevedo said. "We've talked about it in here. We've also talked about why it's okay to talk about it." He paused. "Unfortunately, I do think there's a good chance they'll come down hard on you."

"What will they do?" Grace asked.

Mr. Acevedo pulled back his hair.

"What will they do?" Attie pressed.

"Graduation's untouchable," he said. "I wouldn't worry about that."

"What should we worry about?" Avery asked.

"Everything else," Mr. Acevedo said. "I think everything else is on the table."

"What do you mean, everything else?" Mariam said.

"Gala25?" Danny held his head. "That'd be messed up, Mr. A."

"You're telling me," Noah said.

"Would they really not let us go to Gala25?" Grace asked.

"I think it's a distinct possibility," Mr. Acevedo said.

I gripped the back of my neck. Mr. Acevedo was saying all the same things Mom had said. I felt like I was reliving the car conversation all over again.

"Yo, I don't think they'll do a thing to us," Diego said.

"I wouldn't be so sure, Diego," Mr. Acevedo said.

"We have to stick together," Attie said.

"Strength in numbers, Attie Silverman," Red said.

"I can't believe they'd keep us from going to Gala25," Grace said.

"That would mean no Hoops Machine," Xander said.

"Hoops Machine?" about half the class said at the same time.

I looked down and twisted a lock near my forehead at its root. I didn't want anyone to see that I knew.

"Yeah, Hoops Machine," X said. "Hoops Machine is performing."

"They are," Attie said, nodding. "Hoops Machine is part of Gala25."

The secret was out. Everyone now knew about Hoops Machine. Everyone now knew there was a good chance we'd all miss out. But I was going to miss out more than anyone. Everyone didn't know that. Everyone didn't know I was going to be the unhappiest one of all. I let out a puff. Mom had to be wrong. How could she know for sure they wouldn't let me play?

"I can't believe none of you knew about Hoops Machine," X said. "I'm always the last one to find out about anything around here. I thought for sure—"

"We wanted it to be a surprise," Attie interrupted. "But we knew it would be next to impossible because so many people knew about it. You have no idea how hard we worked . . ." She smacked her leg.

I gripped the back of my neck again, and with my basketball eyes, I looked at Red. He was spinning his movie ticket on his leg. Graduation meant so much to Suzanne, so much. Mom wasn't wrong about that. There was a chance this could ruin everything. Red wasn't going to get to play with Hoops Machine, either. I peeked over at Avery. She was going to miss out, too.

"It's okay, Mason Irving," Red said, putting his hand on my back and leaning forward so I could see his face. "It's okay."

"Thanks, Red," I said.

"I'm so mad at Ms. Darling," Piper said. "How could she do this to us?"

"This isn't Ms. Darling's doing," Mr. Acevedo said. "I wouldn't be too angry with her. She's in a pickle."

"A pickle?" Red said. "Ms. Darling's in a pickle?"

"It's an expression," I said, glancing back. "She's caught in the middle of something."

"Got it," Red said. "Thanks, Mason Irving."

"Elephant and Pickle," Diego said, smiling and bobbing. "Instead of Elephant and Piggie, Elephant and Pickle. Get it?"

Everyone stared.

He shrugged. "Yo, I thought it was funny."

"What kind of pickle, Diego?" Declan asked, grinning. "Half-sour or sour?"

Lots of kids laughed.

"Let's wrap this conversation up," Mr. Acevedo said, tapping the rug. "But I want to share one more thing before we do."

"We're not backing down." Avery rolled forward. "We can do this."

"Yes, you can," Mr. Acevedo said, smiling. "You sure can. You're all capable of doing anything you set your minds to."

Once again, I thought about what Ruiz had said about trusting my instincts, following my heart, and being true to myself. This was the right thing to do. No matter the consequences.

"I want to share our last equation," Mr. Acevedo said, pulling the remote from his pocket and pointing it at the board.

"Luck equals preparation plus opportunity," I said.

A moment later, the words appeared on the board. The kids from the Book Stairs meeting looked my way.

"Luck is what happens when preparation meets opportunity," Mr. Acevedo said. "Often, we create our own luck, and when we do—when preparation and opportunity come together—we seize the moment."

"Yo, we're seizing the moment," Diego said. "We're going rogue!"

Red raised his hand.

"Yes, Red," Mr. Acevedo said.

"What do you think we should do, Mr. Acevedo?"

"What do I think?" Mr. Acevedo placed his hand over his chest and looked at me. "I'll tell you something this first-year teacher learned. You have to pick your battles. That's not always easy. It's almost never easy."

I stared back. It was almost as if Mom had somehow momentarily body-snatched Mr. Acevedo and channeled her words and thoughts through him.

"Whatever you decide to do," Mr. Acevedo said, "whatever choice you make at this point, you have my respect." He drew a perfect circle in the air with his finger, and then, one by one, made eye contact with each of us. "You got people talking, you got people thinking. I'm incredibly proud of all of you."

Confirmation

"It's funny you're reading that," I said to Avery.

She shot me a look. "What?"

"You're reading *Roller Girl*." I pointed to her book, open and facedown next to her on the couch cushion. "That's funny."

"What's funny about it?"

I smiled. "Well, you're a roller girl, right?"

"Whatever, dude," she said. "That's not what the book is about."

Avery and I were the only ones in Room 208. Right before heading down to lunch, Mr. Acevedo had asked me to stay behind and wait for him to come back up.

Now I was buggin'. Well, I had been ever since CC. Make that, I had been ever since yesterday's car ride. The only thing keeping me from completely losing it was Avery. She stayed behind because she told Mr. Acevedo she was too heated to be around people, especially the little kids in the cafeteria.

I climbed into her chair and wheeled across the carpet. "I'm taking your ride for a spin," I said.

"Are you friggin' kidding me?" she said. "Get out of my chair."

I stopped in front of the cubbies and turned around. "I'm so good at this now," I said, grinning. "Hunter was clueless the other day."

"Bring it back, Rip."

I ride in Avery's chair all the time. Okay, maybe not all the time, but I do ride in it.

"Bring it back! Stop being a jerk, Rip."

"Stop being a jerk, Rip," I said, imitating her. "You used to hate my guts. Remember that?"

"Dude, why are you being like this?"

"You did." I spun a half turn and backed to the edge of the carpet. "You used to hate everyone's guts."

"Rip!" She smacked the cushion.

"Teach me how to do that wheelie thing you do," I said.

"I'm not teaching you anything."

"I also want to learn how to hockey-stop. That move is tight."

"Why are you being like this?" she said again.

"I'm trying to cheer you up." I backed into the bathtub. "I think it's working."

"Working? Are you friggin'—"

"I'm trying reverse psychology." I laughed.

Avery looked away. I could see she was trying not to smile.

"Ha!" I pointed. "It is working!"

"What's working?" Mr. Acevedo said, walking in. "What are you two smiling about?"

"Dude, give me back my ride," Avery said.

I popped out of the chair and danced the Carlton. Then I rolled the wheelchair back to Avery.

"I was trying to get her out of her mood," I said. "My charming personality was working."

"Whatever." She slid into her chair and grabbed her book. "I'm out of here. I'll be in Ms. Yvonne's room."

"You can stay," Mr. Acevedo said. "I only need a few minutes with—"

"No, thank you." Avery waved and wheeled out of the room.

Mr. Acevedo sat down cross-legged on the front table and folded his hands in his lap.

"Uh-oh," I said.

He motioned me to the table. I sat down facing him.

"Let's talk about Hoops Machine," he said.

"I can't play if I don't take the test, right?" I said.

"That's right," he said. "You can't."

I punched the table. "That's not right, Mr. Acevedo."

"I don't think it is either, Rip."

I pursed my lips and squinched up my face. Even though I'd known the news was coming, it didn't make hearing it any easier. Confirmation made it worse.

"Do they think . . ." My voice cracked. "They think you're behind it, don't they?"

"No," Mr. Acevedo said.

"Yes, they do."

Mr. Acevedo smiled. "Only some of them. Not all."

"So we are getting you in trouble?"

"I'm fine, Rip." Mr. Acevedo tucked his hair behind his ears. "I appreciate your thoughtfulness."

"I can't believe our last week at RJE . . . I can't believe any of this."

"It is unfortunate."

"Avery was going to play with Hoops Machine," I said.

"Avery?" Mr. Acevedo sat back on his hands.

"She started playing basketball. Red said she's really good."

"Wow," he said. "That's outstanding."

"If she got to play with Hoops Machine, do you know how much that would mean to . . ." I stopped. I would've started crying if I'd finished the sentence.

"You had a lot to do with that." Mr. Acevedo tapped my knee.

"With what?"

"Getting Avery to play," he said. "You know that, right?"

I shrugged.

"You did, Rip. You made a difference in a lot of lives this year. Don't lose sight of that."

I let out a puff. "Do I still go to practice this afternoon?"

"Why wouldn't you?" he said. "Nothing's happened yet, right?" He tapped my knee again. "I expect you to go out there and play the best basketball you've ever played."

Hoops Machine,
Practice Three

I pulled the blue pinnie over my head and raced onto the court. I was scrimmaging with Hoops Machine. That's right, I was on a basketball court scrimmaging with Hoops Machine.

I pinched my arm like I had at each of the first two practices.

I was on Blue Crew with Ruiz, Croft, Groll, Rekate, and Bray. Mega-Man was on Red Crew with Wicks, Gersh, Sinanis, Bailey, and Skeggs.

I waved to Mega-Man, who was jumping in place across the court. He waved back with both hands.

Mega-Man had been the last one to arrive at practice. Ruiz didn't start warm-ups until he did, but as soon as he set foot in the gym, she blew her whistle and got things going. Mega-Man almost face-planted shuffling onto the court wearing his half-on and untied sneakers.

During the drills, Ruiz was all business. We rehearsed

all the routines and practiced the transitions from one segment to the next. Every so often, Ruiz stopped to point something out, test a tweak, ask for a suggestion, or review Plan B. Plan B was what to do if something didn't go as expected at a particular point. Plan B was how to get back in sync smoothly and quickly.

When we finished, it was on to scrimmaging. Right now, I was on a court about to run ball with Hoops Machine. I heard Mr. Acevedo's words:

I expect you to go out there and play the best basketball you've ever played.

I thumped my chest.

* * *

"Here we go, here we go, here we go," Ruiz said, high-stepping and bouncing as she dribbled up the court. "Ball's in."

We were on offense. I was on the wing outside the three-point line. Skeggs was guarding me and giving me space. When Ruiz crossed midcourt, she passed to me and . . . the ball sailed clean through my hands. I didn't even get a finger on it. It hit the wall behind the scorer's table on a fly and bounced straight back to Skeggs.

"I'll take that," she said. She backpedaled to the sideline

and inbounded to Gersh. "The Force may not be with you, Jedi," she said, running at me.

"We're already in his head," Bailey called from the far side of the court. He pointed at me. "We got you."

"Keep your focus, keep your focus." Ruiz clapped hard and looked my way.

I was guarding Skeggs. She set up in the corner, and each time she jab-stepped or faked a cut, she slapped away my hands and bumped me with a forearm or shoulder.

"Hope your defense is better than your offense, Jedi," she said.

Skeggs wasn't beating me. No way. My eyes were glued to her belly button. She wasn't getting past me.

"Back screen, back screen!" Ruiz called.

I felt for Gersh setting a pick behind me.

Bailey whipped a pass to Skeggs, but she didn't catch it. Instead, she touch-passed it right to Mega-Man, who'd rolled off Sinanis's screen and was cutting down the lane. He caught the ball and flipped up a sweet layup.

"That's how to finish!" Bailey double high-fived Mega-Man.

"Every time," Skeggs said, skipping back on defense and staring at me. "You're making this too easy, Jedi."

"What say you, Rip," Croft said, rolling onto the court and rotating in for Bray. "Time to get your game on."

I shook out my dreads. I needed to get my game on fast. If I didn't, this experience was going to change the trajectory of my basketball life, but not in a good way.

"Here we go," Croft added. "These are your middle school tryouts."

My eyes shot to him. I hadn't told anyone on Hoops Machine about middle school basketball. How did he know about tryouts?

Our offense went to work. Ruiz passed to Croft on the far side. He wheeled at Sinanis, who was guarding him, and then swung the ball to Groll in the corner. Groll took a quick shot. It clanked off the back iron. Skeggs grabbed the rebound.

"Every time," she said, smiling as she dribbled upcourt. "Let's do this again, Mega-Man."

I picked up Skeggs near half-court and tried steering her left. Once again, my eyes were fixed on her belly button. As she crossed the time line, she picked up her dribble and in one motion rocket-fired a long two-handed chest pass that hit Mega-Man in stride as he sliced toward the basket. He sank a second, wide-open sweet layup.

"Yes!" Mega-Man cheered. He ran back downcourt, pumping his fists over his head. "Yes!"

"Time to get down to business," Bray said, jogging back onto the court and subbing in for Groll. "Head in the game, Rip."

But my head wasn't in the game. I was thinking about middle school basketball tryouts. I was thinking about the boycott. I was thinking about not playing with Hoops Machine at Gala25. I was thinking about Red missing out on . . .

"Focus, focus," I said, bopping the side of my head. "Full-throttle basketball mode."

I couldn't let Skeggs beat me again. I couldn't let her get another assist. This time down the floor, I couldn't let her touch the ball.

But she still found a way to help Red Crew score. She set the screen for Sinanis, which freed him for a wide-open jumper from the elbow.

I clasped my hands behind my head. How could I not be in basketball mode? How could my brain be thinking about middle school basketball and the boycott and Gala25 and Red and . . .

Doink!

You ever see one of those sports movies where all the action is taking place at full speed, but one player is just standing there in the middle of it doing nothing, and you think that's so unrealistic because something like that would never happen in real life?

Well, something like that does happen in real life. It happened to me. I'd stopped in the middle of the court. I'd stopped in the middle of the action. I was just standing there, and a ball hit me on the side of my head.

Doink!

"Hoops Skywalker putting on a show!" Wicks said, imitating the way Ruiz had said it last week.

Everyone laughed.

Mega-Man

"How cool was that!" Mega-Man said, banging his heel against the side of the curb.

"Pretty cool," I said.

"Pretty cool?" Mega-Man looked at me. "Rip, that was amazing!"

We were sitting along the curb in front of the athletic center. Even though it was dark out, the super-bright LED parking lot lights made it seem like it was the middle of the afternoon. A few of the Hoops Machine players were on the steps behind us farther up the walkway, so it wasn't like we were sitting outside by ourselves.

"The only bad thing about practice was that I walked in late," Mega-Man said. "That was so embarrassing."

"You weren't late," I said. "You were right on time."

"Nuh-uh." Mega-Man shook his head.

"Practice started at six-thirty," I said. "You were there at—"

"That's right," Mega-Man said, cutting me off. "Practice

started at six-thirty. That means I needed to be ready to play at six-thirty. I wasn't ready. I was late." He picked at the grass growing out of the crack in the curb. "My dad used to say that."

"What?"

"My dad used to say that all the time," he said. "If you're

not ready to play at the start of practice, you're late for practice."

I thought about Mega-Man's dad. I don't call him Coach Crazy anymore. I wish I never had.

"Who's picking you up?" Mega-Man asked.

"My mom," I said. "She should be here any sec. What about you?"

"My aunt," Mega-Man said. "She's a vet over—"

"The one you were telling us about?"

"Yeah!" Mega-Man bounced. "My aunt Cheryl."

During the basketball tournament over Easter break, Mega-Man, Diego, Red, and I shared a hotel room. He told us all about his aunt who was a veterinarian.

"You were supposed to work with her over vacation, right?" I said.

"I only got to for a day," he said. "Because my dad had a heart attack."

I swallowed. "I know."

"He almost died."

He almost died.

The words doinked me like that basketball had during the scrimmage. Only harder and head-on. I thought about my dad, what it would be like if that happened to him. I started to shake. I gripped the back of my neck and squeezed it hard.

"I had . . . I had such a good time that night in the hotel," I said, peeking over at Mega-Man.

"That night was amazing." Mega-Man smiled. "It was one of the best nights of my life."

"Yeah." I picked at the grass in the curb. "Hey, um . . . sorry about your dad."

"Thanks. He's getting out of the hospital soon."

"Will he be out in time to see you play with Hoops Machine?"

"My mom told me not to get my hopes up," Mega-Man said. "I'm just glad he's coming home soon."

"It must be . . ." I didn't finish.

"I wasn't going to play," Mega-Man said. "When my mom told me about Hoops Machine, I didn't want to do it. I didn't want to do anything. I kind of still don't. But when I found out you were playing, I . . . I decided to. Thanks, Rip."

I put my hand on Mega-Man's back.

Luke Skywalker

"Welcome to Groovy Movie Tuesday!" Mr. Acevedo said. He leaped onto the table where Olivia, Mariam, and Grace usually sat and pressed the power button on the projector hanging from the ceiling.

The OMG girls were on the couch. Mr. Acevedo said we could sit wherever we wanted today, and since that's where they sat when they walked in this morning, that's where they stayed. Gavin, Hunter, Sebi, and Miles snagged the beanbags, Attie and Melissa jumped in the bathtub, and Diego, X, Red, and I sat on the windowsill.

"I told you yesterday this was going to be one of your favorite classes of the year," Mr. Acevedo said, still standing on the table, "and I meant it."

"It'd better live up to the hype," Diego said, bobbing his head and grinning.

"Hold up." Mr. Acevedo leaped from the front table to the table by the window and looked down at Diego. "You doubting me?"

Red hunched his shoulders and began pinky-thumb-tapping his legs.

"We never doubt you," I said, smiling and bobbing like Diego.

When I'd gotten home from practice the night before, I hadn't thought I'd be able to sleep, not after my disastrous performance in the scrimmage. But I crashed as soon as my head hit my pillow.

This morning, I was still kicking myself over how I played and buggin' over the boycott and maybe missing out on Hoops Machine, but for some reason, I was feeling pretty good. I'm sure nine hours of sleep had something to do with it. I think the conversation with Mega-Man did, too.

"This will be one of your favorite classes of the year," Mr. Acevedo said. "Guaranteed." He drew a perfect circle in the air with his finger. "I'm glad everyone had their tickets."

Mr. Acevedo was also part of why I was feeling pretty good. When we got to Room 208 this morning, he was sitting on his stool in the hallway, collecting tickets. Everyone had to smile and say, "I am in the spirit of Groovy Movie Tuesday" before entering.

"You really wouldn't have let us in without a ticket?" Lana said.

"He wasn't leaving anyone out today," Danny said. "No way."

"Luckily, we didn't have to find out," Mr. Acevedo said.

"Since it's Groovy Movie Tuesday," Trinity said, "does that mean we're seeing a movie from the sixties or seventies?"

"Yeah, spill it, Teach," Declan said. "What movie are we seeing?"

"Can we watch one of the Toy Story movies?" Melissa asked before Mr. Acevedo could answer. "Or *Big Hero 6*? I love that movie."

"If we're watching something animated," Zachary said, "we have to watch Miyazaki. *Spirited Away* or *Howl's Moving Castle*."

"I say we watch a Star Wars movie," Noah said. "Just not *The Phantom Menace*."

Attie stood up in the bathtub. "Why don't we watch—"

"Whoa, whoa, whoa!" Mr. Acevedo said, cutting her off and waving his arms like a ref waving off a basket. "I'm in charge here. I make the call." He pointed his index fingers at Noah. "Believe it or not, we are watching Star Wars."

"Seriously?" Noah pumped a fist.

Seriously was right. At basketball, everyone was calling me Hoops Skywalker and young Jedi, and now in class, it was more Star Wars.

"Please tell me we're watching *The Empire Strikes Back*," Noah said. "That's the best one by far."

"Definitely," Hunter said. "Either *The Empire Strikes*

Back or *Revenge of the Sith*. That movie is so much better than people—"

"*Return of the Jedi*," X said. "I don't care what anyone says. I love the Ewoks. The Ewoks are—"

"Take a breath, everyone." Mr. Acevedo waved his arms again. "I said I'm in charge here." He patted his chest. "Give me a sec. Let me cue things up."

* * *

Do you know how you know you have the coolest teacher of all time? When the *Star Wars* opening credits begin, he stands at the front of the room and pretends he's conducting the orchestra. Then he starts humming along like he's almost singing, and then before you know it, the whole class is humming and singing. Even the fourth graders passing in the hall stop to join in.

That's how you know. I hope I have teachers like Mr. Acevedo next year.

We didn't watch all of *Star Wars*. We watched two clips. The first one was from the original *Star Wars*. It was the early scene on Tatooine, when Luke and Uncle Owen buy C-3PO and R2-D2.

Noah knew every line.

"But I was going into Tosche Station to pick up some

power converters," he said, whining the words exactly the way Luke did.

The second clip was from *Return of the Jedi*. It was the big scene toward the end when Luke takes on Darth Vader and Darth Sidious.

"Never!" a few of the kids and Mr. Acevedo shouted when Luke tossed away his lightsaber and refused to kill his father.

Like I said, the coolest teacher of all time.

* * *

"Let's talk character," Mr. Acevedo said. He sat cross-legged on the front table, holding both ankles. "When we discuss books in here, we talk a lot about characters, especially how they grow and develop over the course of a story. Let's do the same with the characters in another form of art, film."

"This sounds so dope," Attie said.

"It is." Mr. Acevedo rocked back and forth. "To show we understand what we read, we use our minds. We think, we reflect, we analyze, and we discuss. We share examples to support our understanding. We're going to do the same thing with the characters from these two Star Wars clips. Let me give you the guidelines."

"Do we need to write down our answers?" Piper asked.

"Let me explain the assignment," Mr. Acevedo said.

"Well, I can't exactly call this an assignment. It's an activity. It will probably be easier for those of you who haven't seen the movies, because we're not using prior knowledge. We're only focusing on these two clips, and we're only focusing on Luke."

"We're comparing him in the two clips?" Olivia asked.

"That's exactly what we're doing," Mr. Acevedo said. "Think about how he's grown and developed. How has he changed? And as we're doing this, think in terms of show, don't tell. Show the examples of how he's changed."

"Can we work with someone?" I asked.

"You can work by yourself, with a partner, or in a small group," Mr. Acevedo said.

Red and I topped fists.

* * *

Red and Rip
Tuesday, June 10
Mr. Acevedo

Comparing Luke Skywalker

In *Star Wars*
- Acts like a teenager when Uncle Owen tells him to take the droid

- Doesn't want to do his chores
- Wants to hang out with his friends
- Tone of voice, the way he talks
- Whiny, spoiled

In *Return of the Jedi*
- Doesn't listen to Darth Sidious
- He tosses the lightsaber
- "Never!"
- Stands up for himself
- His own person
- Fights his own battles
- Mature
- Brave

* * *

"Who wants to start us off?" Mr. Acevedo asked.

Avery pushed her wheels hard and rolled to the whiteboard.

"I guess Avery does," Mr. Acevedo said. He gave her a pound. "You could've stayed over there."

"Whatever." She shrugged.

"What do you got?" Mr. Acevedo said. "Share an example of character growth."

"In the first clip," Avery said, "Luke was acting like a

friggin' brat. All he wanted to do was hang out with his friends. He talked whiny and annoying."

"That's exactly what we wrote," Red whispered.

"In the other scene," Avery said, "he sounded different. He was much more grown-up. And confident. Especially taking on Darth Sidious."

"Nice, Avery," Mr. Acevedo said.

"Who else wants to share?" Avery said, imitating him. She brushed hair off her face and then tucked some strands behind her ears.

"You making fun of me?" Mr. Acevedo gave her a look.

"Maybe." She stared back and pretended to adjust her earrings.

Everyone laughed.

"Keep it up," Mr. Acevedo said.

Avery pointed to Sebi. "What did you come up with?"

"I drew pictures of Luke," he said, holding up his sketch pad.

"That's outstanding!" Mr. Acevedo said.

Sebi is an unbelievable artist. You should see the gargoyles and zombies he drew for the comic he and Miles made.

"This is what Luke looked like in the *Star Wars* scene." He tapped one of the drawings. "His hair was floppy and messy. And this is what he looked like in *Return of the Jedi*." He pointed to the other picture. "His hair was shorter and neater. He looked more like an adult."

"Excellent, Sebi," Avery said, still acting like Mr. Acevedo. "Anyone else?" She nodded to Diego.

"In the first clip," he said, "when Luke waved the smoke out of his face after the red droid blew up, he looked like he just smelled a nasty fart."

Everyone laughed.

"Yo, he did." Diego bobbed his head and grinned. "Tell me I'm wrong."

Avery pointed to Olivia, sitting on the couch's armrest.

"We noticed that the way he moved changed," she said, motioning to Mariam and Grace. "In *Star Wars*, he ran like a boy. He was almost skipping. Then in *Revenge of the Jedi*, he did that—"

"Return!" a bunch of kids said.

"It's *Return of the Jedi*," Melissa said. "Not *Revenge of the Jedi*."

"Not true," Noah said. "It was originally called *Revenge of the Jedi*. In the first teaser, it was called *Revenge of the Jedi*."

"One of my brothers has a *Revenge of the Jedi* poster," X said.

"Can I say our answer?" Olivia waved her paper. "In the first one, he ran and skipped like a kid. In the second one, he did that backflip."

"He was using the Force," Noah said.

"He looked like a gymnast," Olivia said. "That had to be a stuntman."

"My answer is a little different," Attie said, standing in the tub again.

Avery and Mr. Acevedo pointed to her. He hip-bumped her armrest.

"Luke is all about family," Attie said. "In the *Star Wars* clip, he listens to his uncle even though he wants to do something else. In the *Return of the Jedi* scene, he refuses to kill his father, Darth Vader. He puts his family first. Luke's feelings change, but what's in his heart doesn't."

"Outstanding!" Mr. Acevedo air-high-fived her from across the room. "When we read, we make text-to-self connections. Let's make some film-to-self connections. How does what we just watched and discussed apply to us?"

Red's hand shot up. Mr. Acevedo called on him.

"At the beginning of the school year," Red said, clenching his fists and tapping his legs, "Avery Goodman never participated. Now Avery Goodman participates all the time. At the beginning of the year . . . at the beginning of the year, Sebastian King didn't share his drawings. Now Sebastian King shares his drawings all the time. At the beginning of the year—"

"Let me stop you right there, Red," Mr. Acevedo said. He bounded over and gave him a double pound. "You absolutely nailed it. Way to go!"

"Thanks, Mr. Acevedo!"

Mr. Acevedo faced the class. "You're not the same kids

you were when you walked into Room 208 back in September," he said. He patted his chest. "At your core, you are, but you've all grown. You're all more mature."

"I'm mature?" Diego said. "Tell that to my moms."

Mr. Acevedo smiled. "The same goes for me," he said. "I'm not the same teacher I was when I first set foot in Room 208 back in September. I've grown, too." He drew a perfect circle in the air with his finger. "We've grown together, we've learned together. That's what we did this year. As a classroom community, we made learning our priority."

Boycott Eve

After dinner, I went right out to the driveway to work on my dribbling. I took two basketballs so I could do windshield wipers. Coach Acevedo loved that dribbling drill because it was great for ball control, touch, and timing. It also worked both hands equally.

When it was almost completely dark, Mom finally came outside.

"Honey, we need to talk about tomorrow," she said, walking down the driveway.

I kept on dribbling. I knew she'd come out to get me eventually, but I'd thought it was going to be sooner. We hadn't spoken much since the car ride conversation on Sunday. Mom worked late yesterday, and at dinner tonight, we only made small talk about the NBA finals, how hot and humid it was, and Bubba's vet appointment next week.

"I'd like for you to come inside, Rip," she said.

The ball I was dribbling with my left hand kicked off my foot and rolled onto the grass.

"Dag." I rapped my leg. "Why, Mom? Why do we have to talk about tomorrow?"

She picked up the ball and dribbled back over. "Honey, you don't know what I want to say."

"Yeah, I do," I said.

But to be perfectly honest, I didn't, and her tone was nothing like in the car the other day. She spoke like she wanted to have an actual conversation.

"Rip, I know you've given this a lot of thought," she said. "I know this isn't something—"

"Then why do we have to keep on talking about it?"

"Can you lose the attitude?" she said, pinching her finger and thumb together. "A teeny-tiny bit?"

"I don't have an attitude."

"You have an attitude."

I had an attitude. I definitely had an attitude. I really didn't want to talk about tomorrow. I just wanted tomorrow to happen.

"We've been through this, Mom," I said, losing the attitude a teeny-tiny bit. "I understand everything about tomorrow."

"I just want to make sure you—"

"Mom, stop." I trapped the basketball I'd been holding under my foot. "I know, I do. I know how much this means to Red and Suzanne. I do, I get it. And I know how much of a you-know-what show this makes for you at your school."

"That's for sure," she said. She dribbled the ball behind her back a few times and then faked a one-handed pass to me. Then she faked another. "My handle's still better than yours."

"Whatever," I said.

"Honey, I am proud of you," she said, sitting down on her ball and motioning to the driveway.

"You have a funny way of showing it." I sat down on my ball facing her.

"I'm sorry about the car ride the other day." She touched my leg. "I wish I'd handled that differently."

"Thanks," I said softly. "You were upset."

"I still wish you weren't doing it," she said. "You're not exactly making life easy."

"I never do."

I kicked out my legs, planted my heels, and rolled around on my basketball. Mom started rolling around on hers, too. I thought back to the school-yard last week,

when Red and I were sitting on our basketballs talking about middle school tryouts. It seemed so long ago.

"My little activist!" Mom reached over and ruffled my hair.

I ducked away. My mom never ruffled my hair. Never. It was odd that she had.

"I learned from the best," I said.

"That's right, you did," she said. "Don't you forget it."

"Never."

"It takes courage to stand up for what you believe in," she said. "Guts. But listen, my little rabble-rouser, real activism comes with real risk and real costs." She pointed at my eyes. "Never lose sight of that. It keeps you focused."

I thought about Ruiz. I could hear her telling me the same thing.

Mom motioned to my hair. "Those need to be relocked," she said. "You're not going to graduation with—"

"If I go to graduation," I said, shaking out my dreads.

"You're going to graduation." She picked a piece of lint from above my ear. "You're not going to graduation with ratty hair."

"I'm cutting it soon," I said.

"That's what you've been saying."

"Before middle school starts." I pulled at the locks near my forehead at their root. "Before basketball tryouts."

She put her hand on my knee. "You do understand, whatever happens tomorrow, you're on your own with this."

"I know."

"I won't be able to rescue you," she said. "We're going to have to live with the consequences."

"I know," I said again.

"You're sure Red's okay?"

"Is he getting a dog for graduation?"

"What?" She made a face—too much of a face.

"Ha!" I pointed. "I knew it!"

"Knew what?" she said.

"He is getting a dog for graduation!"

"I don't know what you're talking about," she said, shaking her head.

Yes, she did. She knew exactly what I was talking about. I knew Mom's faces.

"Look at Bubba," I said, pointing to the house.

Bubba was watching us out the front window.

"That dog can't take her eyes off you," Mom said.

"She's the greatest graduation present of all time."

"We thought you'd think so. And I just love watching you with her." She gave me a tap. "Okay, now I have one last thing I need to say."

"It's going to be principally, right?"

She smiled. "Very principally."

"Okay, let's hear it."

"Honey, what you're doing tomorrow is a big deal," she said. "A very big deal. But I want you to keep a little perspective here. This is fifth grade. We're only talking about fifth-grade graduation." She squeezed my knee again. "No matter what happens with all this, it isn't going to make or break you, but it will help shape you."

Red Being Red

"I bet you I know something about Rip Hamilton you don't," Red said as we walked along Key Place on our way to school the next morning.

"I bet you don't," I said.

"I bet you I do, Mason Irving."

I may have been having a conversation with Red, but I was thinking about the boycott. In less than an hour, I'd be sitting in Room 208 with my classmates, refusing to take a test.

"Go," I said. "Tell me something I don't know about Rip Hamilton."

"Rip Hamilton was the first player in the history of the National Basketball Association to lead his team in scoring in a game without scoring a single field goal," he said.

I didn't know that. I gave Red a playful shove. He pushed me back.

"In a game against the Memphis Grizzlies," Red said,

"Rip Hamilton led the Detroit Pistons in scoring with fourteen points, but Rip Hamilton didn't score a single field goal. Rip Hamilton missed all ten of his field goals. But Rip Hamilton made all fourteen of his free throws."

"I bet you don't know who won the game," I said.

"The Memphis Grizzlies won the game," Red said, grinning. "The Memphis Grizzlies defeated the Detroit Pistons, 101–79."

At the corner of Niagara Drive, Red spun around the stop sign. Red spins around all the stop signs and streetlights on the walk to school.

Red wasn't thinking about the test. Or the boycott. Or Gala25. Or Hoops Machine. Or graduation. At the moment, the only thing that mattered to Red was this walk to school.

In other words, Red was being Red.

"I bet you I know something else about Rip Hamilton you don't," he said.

"I bet you don't."

"I bet you I do, Mason Irving," he said. "It's something about Rip Hamilton from when he was younger."

"He went to Coatesville Area High in Pennsylvania," I said. "Is that what you were going to tell me?"

"No."

Up ahead, I could see the entrance to the schoolyard.

"He played AAU summer ball with Kobe Bryant," I said.
"That's not it either."

"When he was at the University of Connecticut, he—"

"It's about Rip Hamilton's nickname," he interrupted.

I flinched. "What?"

"It's about Rip Hamilton's nickname," Red said again.

I swallowed. "What about it?"

"Rip Hamilton's father was nicknamed Rip, too. Rip Hamilton's father passed the nickname down to his son."

"That's cool," I said. "I didn't know that."

Red laughed. "Rip Hamilton's father got the nickname from his mother because he always ripped off his diapers."

I wobbled. "What?"

"Rip Hamilton's father got the nickname—"

"No," I said, cutting him off. "I heard you."

"Rip Hamilton's father always ripped off his diapers!" Red said, laughing.

We got our nicknames the same way, the *exact* same way. I gripped the back of my neck. Mom and Dad had to know. Or did they?

"Rip Hamilton's father passed the nickname on to his son because every superstar needs a nickname," Red said.

I stopped a few steps from the schoolyard entrance.

"Every superstar does need a nickname," I said. "That's why my name . . ."

I didn't finish. I didn't tell Red about my nickname.

"It's time to boycott a test," I said instead. I held out my fist.

Red gave me a pound. "Oh, yeah, Mason Irving," he said. "It's time to boycott a test."

Bubbling the Bubble

I tapped my pencil against my leg. Room 208 was in full-throttle testing mode. The walls were covered in brown paper, the meeting-area furniture was pushed against the cubbies, and we were all sitting in rows. I was in the last seat of the first row by the YO! READ THIS! board.

I checked my classmates. Everyone was in on the boycott. Everyone.

Strength in numbers.

"At this time," Mr. Acevedo said, "all students should have two sealed testing booklets and one sealed scan sheet. Check to make sure you have these materials."

He stood at the front of Room 208 as he read from the instructions, sounding official and like anything but our Mr. Acevedo.

I glanced at the testing monitor seated in front of the Swag Corner. She had her laptop open and a yellow legal pad next to it. I'd never seen her before. She looked like Edna Mode from *The Incredibles*.

Step by step, Mr. Acevedo continued to recite the instructions—unseal the scan sheet, remove the scan sheet from the plastic, place the plastic on the floor underneath our seats.

"Do not unseal either testing booklet until you are instructed to do so," he said for at least the fifth or sixth time.

Diego raised his hand.

"Yes, Diego?" Mr. Acevedo said.

"Should we unseal our booklets?" he said, grinning.

Mr. Acevedo half smiled. "Check the information at the top of your scan sheet," he said. "Check to make sure your name and date of birth are correct. I will give you a moment to check this information."

My name and date of birth were correct.

"At the bottom of your scan sheet, there is a ten-digit identification number. Check to make sure the ten-digit identification number matches the ten-digit identification number on the back of each of your two sealed testing booklets. I will give you a moment to check this information."

My identification numbers matched.

"At this time," Mr. Acevedo said, "does anyone have any questions?"

Attie raised her hand.

"Yes, Attie?" he said.

"I don't have a question," she said. "I have a statement. I'm refusing to take the test. I bubbled in the opt-out circle on my scan sheet."

Mr. Acevedo smiled. Well, he didn't really smile, but I've been around Mr. Acevedo long enough to know when he's smiling on the inside even when he's not showing it on the outside.

Everyone in Room 208 knows it.

Diego raised his hand.

"Yes, Diego?" Mr. Acevedo said.

"Yo, I'm refusing to take the test," he said. "I bubbled in the circle on my scan sheet."

Xander's hand went up.

"Yes, X?" Mr. Acevedo said.

"Me, too," he said. "I'm refusing to take the test. I bubbled in the circle on my scan sheet."

Grace raised her hand. Then Hunter raised his hand. Then Trinity, Danny, Zachary, and Mariam all raised their hands. With my basketball eyes, I checked Edna Mode. She was walking her way to the front of the room and staring at Principal Darling. Principal Darling was now standing in the doorway, watching the hands go up.

I bubbled in my scan sheet and raised my hand.

This was happening. This was really happening.

I looked around at all the raised hands. We were doing it. The students in Room 208 were refusing to take the test. We were standing up for what we believed in.

I hadn't been sure what it was going to feel like when the moment finally arrived. I'd known it was going to feel great, but I hadn't realized it would feel this *powerful*.

Strength in numbers.

Fast and Furious

Principal Darling stood at the front of Room 208, where Mr. Acevedo had read us the testing instructions a few hours ago. Mr. Acevedo sat on the windowsill with his arms folded, where I'd sat yesterday during the Star Wars activity.

We weren't allowed to go to recess. After lunch, the whole class had to return to the room. We sat at the desks still arranged in rows, in the same seats we sat in earlier. The kids who went to a separate location for the test were here now, too.

"An e-mail was sent out to all of your parents," Principal Darling said. "Everyone has already responded." She glanced at Edna Mode in the corner. "A follow-up e-mail will be sent out this afternoon. Yes, you will be permitted to attend graduation on Saturday, but you will not be permitted to attend any of the Gala25 festivities on Friday."

I stared at Principal Darling. This wasn't coming from her. This was something she *had* to say.

* * *

As the rest of class headed out for what was left of our second-to-last-ever RJE recess, I stayed at my seat. Principal Darling had told me to stay behind.

"You do understand, Rip," she said, walking up, "you're not permitted to play with Hoops Machine."

I nodded. "I know."

"You're not permitted to attend practice this afternoon," she added.

With my basketball eyes, I checked Edna Mode in the far corner. She was staring right at us. I looked at Mr. Acevedo, too. He was still on the windowsill with his arms folded. He was shaking his head.

"Okay." I gripped the back of my neck. "I have to let Hoops Machine know I won't be there."

"They've already been told," Principal Darling said. "They've already been told you won't be playing with them anymore."

Hoops No More

I sat on my bedroom floor next to Bubba. She was sound asleep on top of the clothes I wore to school. Bubba loves it when I leave my dirty clothes on the floor. She especially loves it when I leave my dirty, sweaty basketball clothes on the floor.

I didn't tonight because I didn't go to basketball. I didn't play with Hoops Machine. That's all I was able to think about, which was why I was sitting on my bedroom floor in the dark at twelve-thirty in the morning.

How were they replacing me in the opening? Was Rekate extending her seated-dribbling bit? Was Croft adding moves and tricks to his routine? Was Bailey lengthening his Carlton dance? Or were they just going to skip my part and pull out a real latecomer like they usually do?

My mind went to Mega-Man. Did he know I wasn't playing anymore? Did they tell me? I thought about what he'd said.

When my mom told me about Hoops Machine, I didn't

want to do it. I didn't want to do anything. I kind of still don't.
But when I found out you were playing, I . . . I decided to.
Thanks, Rip.

I reached for my phone next to Bubba's paw and tapped the screen. The texts with Red from earlier appeared.

Ripster32: im supposed 2 b @ hoops machine right now

BlakeDaniels24: I know.

Ripster32: im missing hoops machine

BlakeDaniels24: Hoops Machine isn't missing you.

BlakeDaniels24: Ha!

Ripster32: ha

I placed my hand on Bubba's belly. She sighed with her whole body.

"You know I'm here, girl," I said. "I know you do."

Last year, in Ms. Wright's class, we had two full sets of the Vet Volunteers books. I read five—*Storm Rescue, Teacher's Pet, End of the Race, Fight for Life,* and *Time to Fly.* We got to watch a vid of Laurie Halse Anderson talking about the series. She said that when you touch your dog, the dog's entire body tingles. Your touch means the world to your dog.

I leaned back and rested my head on Bubba's neck. "I love you, girl," I said.

I stared at my bedroom door. The hallway light was off. Mom had turned it off about an hour ago when she got home. But she didn't come in to check on me. Mom always checks on me when she gets home, even on the nights she comes home super late.

I sighed with my whole body.

Too Harsh

"Really, Rip?" Mom said when she walked into the kitchen the next morning.

I was sitting at the island, eating a bowl of Honey Nut Cheerios, but I only had on my Finn and Jake boxers. That's what prompted her reaction. Mom doesn't like it when I walk

around the house in just my underwear. She hates it when I'm in *her* kitchen in just my underwear.

She pressed the power button on the coffeemaker and opened the fridge.

"You have a meeting?" I asked, swiveling my stool.

The only time Mom makes coffee in the morning—instead of stopping at Perky's—is when she's running late or has a meeting.

She placed a couple Granny Smiths on the counter and shut the fridge. "This is the last time you get away with this," she said, wagging her iPad at my lack of clothes. "I'm not having this over the summer." She sat down beside me and folded her arms.

I put down my spoon. "Uh-oh," I said.

"Yes, uh-oh," she said, nodding. "I couldn't do this to you last night."

"Do what?" I wrapped my ankle around the footrest.

She propped up the iPad so I could see the e-mail on the screen. "I received this yesterday evening," she said. "It's from the school board. It has a lot more to do with me than you."

"What does it say?"

"Next year, the students are no longer eligible to participate in athletics during the first semester," she said, reading from the e-mail. "If the students remain in good standing during the first semester, they will be eligible to participate in athletics during the second semester."

"Wait, what?" I held my head. "What does that mean?"

"It means the school board . . . the school board is piling on," she said.

I wobbled. "I can't play basketball in the fall?"

"That's what they're saying."

"How can . . . how can they do this?" My voice cracked. "Are they allowed to?"

"I'm afraid they are," she said. "They wield quite a bit of power around here."

"How can they do that?" I said. Tears streamed down both my cheeks. "Mom, this is so not fair."

"Incredibly unfair," she said calmly. "It's mean-spirited and unnecessary. Even I didn't expect this level of—"

"Mom, that's the whole class!" I shook my hands.

"I know. It's a lot of kids."

"Have you spoken to other parents?" I asked. "Have you—"

"Rip," she said firmly. She placed her hand on my leg. "I need you to listen. Are you listening?"

"This isn't right, Mom." I wiped my cheeks with my palms. The tears kept coming. "It isn't."

"Are you listening?"

"Why are . . . why are they doing this?" My voice cracked again.

"Honey, I need you to listen."

"I am," I said, nodding and sniffling.

"Remember what I told you the other night," she said. "I said I wasn't going to be able to rescue you. We were going to have to live with the consequences."

"This is different, Mom," I said, folding my arms and pressing them against my chest. "They can't take away middle school basketball."

"Honey, I know. I do. But I need you to keep it together." She tucked some locks behind my ear and then thumb-wiped the tears from under my eyes. "As upset as you are—and you have every right to be—I need you not to lose it." She smiled. "I'm trying my best not to."

I let out a long puff and grimaced.

"You're going to weather this storm, Rip," she said. She placed her hand against my cheek. "You can handle whatever hand you're dealt. I know you can."

"I know," I said softly.

"You're going to be fine," she said. "We both are. We'll get through this together." She sat up and powered down the iPad. "I already texted your father."

"What did he say?" I asked.

"He's ready to hop on a plane and fly halfway around the world," she said.

I managed half a smile. "I'll text him later," I said.

"He wanted me to tell you he's never been more proud of you."

I wiped away a leftover tear with my shoulder.

"Speaking personally," Mom added, "I'm glad he's on the other side of the planet for this." She stood and headed for the coffeemaker. "Your father can have quite the temper when it comes to injustices, especially those involving loved ones."

"I have to go meet Red," I said, spinning off my stool.

"Honey, I need you to trust me on this," she said, filling her thermos. "Do you trust me?"

I nodded.

"Yes?" she said.

"Yes."

"I'm taking you to school this morning," she said. "That's why no Perky's for me."

"What about Red?" I asked.

"Suzanne's driving him."

"Dag," I said. "Red and I walk every day." I let out a puff. "This isn't how RJE is supposed to end."

The Last CC

On my last full day of elementary school, I didn't walk to school with my best friend like I'd done pretty much every day for as long as I could remember. Instead, Mom drove me and dropped me off in the side lot with the rest of the car-rider kids.

As I walked along the front circle toward the main entrance, I stared at the large banner:

GALA 25
Reese Jones Elementary
25th Anniversary Celebration
WELCOME BACK!

* * *

"Next fall," Mr. Acevedo said, "I won't be returning to RJE."

That's how he opened our last CC. We were all in the meeting area. He sat cross-legged on the rug in his usual spot.

"I waited until now to share the news because I didn't want it to be a distraction," Mr. Acevedo said. "I also waited because I didn't know with absolute certainty until yesterday evening."

"You're not coming back because of what the school board did," Danny said.

"No," Mr. Acevedo said.

"Yes, that's why," Avery said.

"No, no, no." Mr. Acevedo wagged a finger. "Believe it or not, their decision had nothing—"

"Whatever, dude," Avery said, not letting him finish. "Not buying it."

I wasn't buying it either, and from the looks on everyone's faces, we weren't the only ones. The whole class knew about what the school board had done. Most had learned about it from their parents. The rest found out when they got to school this morning.

"They're making you leave, aren't they?" Melissa said.

"It's not like that." Mr. Acevedo wagged his finger again. "I made this decision."

"So, then, what's the decision?" Miles asked. "What's the story?"

"I still don't have a definitive plan," he said, "but I know I won't be here next year."

"Are you still going to be a teacher?" Olivia asked.

"Oh, absolutely," he said. "I may be one and done at RJE, but I'm not one and done with education."

I pointed to Ms. Yvonne, sitting between Red and Xander on the couch. "What about you?" I asked. "Are you coming back?"

"I'm not going anywhere," she said.

"Are you moving to another school, Teach?" Declan asked.

"To be determined," Mr. Acevedo answered. "Weighing a few options right now."

"Will you let us know when you decide?" Lana asked.

"You have my word," he said. "I'll still be in the area. I'm not moving, so even if I'm not in the district next—"

"So you might still be in the district?" Trinity interrupted.

"Yo, you're teaching middle school next year?" Diego said.

"Hold on," Mr. Acevedo said, waving his hands. "That's how rumors start. I said no such thing."

"Are you coaching middle school basketball?"

Middle school basketball.

I don't know who asked the question. Hunter? Noah? Danny? It didn't matter. The three words rocked me. I placed my palms on the floor for balance and stared at Mr. Acevedo. Our eyes met. He nodded once.

"Enough about my next year." Mr. Acevedo strummed the floor. "Let's talk about the here and now." He reached back for a picture book.

"Sweet," Diego said. "Story time!"

"Yes and no," Mr. Acevedo said, holding up *Tell Me a Tattoo Story.* "I read this yesterday, and it's inspired me to share one of my tattoo stories." He placed the book on the rug and recrossed his legs. "One of my best friends is Ms. Hamburger's son."

"*The* Ms. Hamburger?" Avery said.

"The Ms. Hamburger," he said. "Her granddaughter, my friend's daughter, is my goddaughter. Got that?" He grabbed his ankles. "My goddaughter has a birthmark on her leg. For the longest time, she was really self-conscious about it. She wouldn't wear shorts. She wouldn't go swimming. She didn't want anyone to see it."

"So you got a tattoo of it," X said.

"Ding, ding, ding." Mr. Acevedo pretended to ring a

bell. "That's exactly what I did." He rolled up his jeans so we could see the multicolored butterfly tats on his leg. "This green one here isn't really a butterfly. This is what her birthmark looks like."

"That's so dope," Attie said. "What made you think of that?"

"I read a post online about a dad who got a tattoo of his daughter's hearing aid," Mr. Acevedo said. "That's what gave me the idea."

Red raised his hand.

"Yes, Red." Mr. Acevedo pointed to him.

"Can we talk about the elephant in the room?" he asked.

Everyone laughed.

"What's the elephant in the room?" Mr. Acevedo asked, smiling.

"It's an expression," Red answered. He tapped his fist on the armrest. "It's what everyone is thinking about, but no one is talking about."

"Yes," Mr. Acevedo said. He rolled his jeans back down and

crossed his legs again. "Let's talk about the elephant in the room."

"Thanks, Mr. Acevedo," Red said.

Mr. Acevedo looked around the meeting area. "I'm sad about Gala25," he said. "I think it's safe to say we all are. But you all understood your actions would have consequences and that you'd have to live with them, unpleasant as they may be."

I twisted a lock near my forehead at its root. Like so many times this year, it was as if Mom had channeled her words and thoughts through some secret educator portal, planted them in Mr. Acevedo's brain, and programmed him to say them.

"I'm deeply disappointed in the board's decision about middle school athletics," he said. He adjusted the hoop in the top of his ear. "I don't understand what purpose it serves. I think it's overly—"

"It's the friggin' worst," Avery said.

"You get no argument from me," Ms. Yvonne said.

"Each and every one of you stood up for what you believed in even though you knew there would be costs involved," he said. He drew a perfect circle in the air around us. "That's admirable. That's impressive."

"You're getting sentimental again, Mr. A.," Zachary said.

"I can't help it." He strummed the carpet and snapped

192

his fingers. "I was able to come up with one last *mi abuela* quote."

"I thought you said you exhausted your supply," Attie said.

"I thought I did," Mr. Acevedo said. "My aunt reminded me of this one: *El éxito en la vida no se mide por lo que logras, sino por los obstaculos que superas.*"

Zachary, Christine, and Isa raised their hands to offer translations.

"I'll translate this last one," Mr. Acevedo said, motioning their hands down. He looked around the meeting area. His eyes stopped on mine. "Success in life is measured not by what you have achieved, but by the obstacles you overcome."

Backyard Again

I lay on the grass with my hands clasped behind my head and watched the blue sky darken. Red was playing with Bubba. Every few moments, the tennis ball would fly past or bounce by. Each time it did, I braced for Bubba impact. Sometimes she charged into me or stepped on me. Other times, she'd jump over or scamper around me. A couple times, she stopped to sniff my crotch or lick my face.

Like right now.

"Good, Bubba Chuck," Red said.

I playfully pushed her tongue away from my mouth. Bubba thought I was playing. Of course, she thought I was playing. Bubba always thinks I'm playing, so she moved in for more licks.

"Get away." I pushed her off with my forearm. "I don't have any carrots, girl. He does."

Red laughed. "Good girl, Bubba Chuck."

Red was trying to cheer me up. He'd been trying all day,

but to be perfectly honest, it had gotten a little annoying, especially now with Bubba barreling into me, stepping on me, and licking me. But Red didn't mean to be annoying.

Red was just being Red.

The tennis ball rolled to a stop against my leg. I grabbed it before Bubba arrived and flung it in Red's direction.

"He's over there." I sat up on my elbows and pushed Bubba away. "How many carrots have you given her?"

"Not that many."

"You're cleaning it up if she makes a mess."

"I'm breaking them into small bits," Red said, jogging over. He held out his hand. "This is two baby carrots, Mason Irving."

Red wasn't breaking the carrots into small bits. He was breaking them into ridiculously tiny bits. There must've been twenty or thirty carrot pieces in his hand.

"When I get my dog," Red said, "I'm going to train her with baby carrots and—"

"Wait, what?" I interrupted. "You're getting a dog?"

"One day," he said. "I hope I get a dog one day."

For a moment, I thought he knew, but he didn't. He still had no idea, which was pretty amazing because Red always senses when something big is up.

"Bubba Chuck and Ambi Turner can have playdates," Red said.

"Ambi Turner?"

"That's what I'm naming my dog," Red said. "I'm naming my dog Ambi Turner."

"I hope she can go left," I said.

"Oh, yeah, Mason Irving," Red said, hopping. "Ambi Turner will definitely be an ambi-turner! When Bubba Chuck and Ambi Turner have playdates, they can play Dog."

"Dog?"

"Dog. When dogs play Horse, they play Dog," Red said, giggling. "Bubba Chuck and Ambi Turner will play Dog."

I popped to my feet and held out my fist. "Nice one," I said.

Red gave me a pound.

With my basketball eyes, I checked Bubba. She was by the steps to the deck, gnawing on the tennis ball.

"Remember yesterday, when you told me about Rip Hamilton's nickname?" I said.

"Rip Hamilton's father was nicknamed Rip because he always ripped off his diapers," Red said. "Rip Hamilton's father passed the nickname down to his son."

"Yeah," I said. "That's how I got my nickname, too."

"You're Rip after Rip Hamilton."

"No," I said. "I thought I was, but I'm not."

"How did you get your nickname, Mason Irving?"

"My dad told me at the tournament over Easter vacation,"

I said. I brushed the locks off my forehead. "I got my nick-name because I used to rip off my diapers and walk around butt naked."

"Wow!" Red hopped from foot to foot. "You got your nicknames the same way. That's the awesomest thing ever!"

"You think?"

"Oh, yeah, Mason Irving," Red said, rapping his knuck-les against his legs. "That's definitely the most awesomest thing ever."

I smiled. I stared at Red. All day long, he'd been trying to cheer me up, make me feel even a little better.

He had.

"Thanks," I said, placing my hand on his shoulder.

"Thanks for what, Mason Irving?"

"Thanks for being who you are," I said.

"Who else would I be?"

Something's Up

The next morning, Red and I didn't walk to school together. On our last-ever day of elementary school, we didn't walk to RJE. Mom drove me again. Suzanne drove Red.

We met up in the side lot and walked along the front circle to the main entrance. But when we reached the building, Ms. Darling wasn't standing between the double doors greeting everyone, and Ms. Waldon wasn't at her desk under the announcement monitor in the main hall. They always were.

"Something's up," Red said.

"Really?" I said. "Thanks for telling me." I bumped his shoulder.

He bumped me back. "You're welcome, Mason Irving."

We two-at-a-timed the Book Stairs and speed-walked down the hall to Room 208, but when we got there, Mr. Acevedo wasn't in the room. Mr. Acevedo was always there when we arrived. The few times he wasn't, Ms. Yvonne was. But she wasn't there either.

Gavin and Miles walked in. Avery rolled in. The OMG girls arrived. But there was still no sign of Mr. Acevedo, and no sign of Ms. Yvonne. More and more kids arrived, and soon the whole class was there except for the teachers.

Everyone was talking. Talking about Gala25 and graduation and Principal Darling and the school board. Everyone was saying what they knew or *thought* they knew. Everyone was saying what they heard from someone or saying what their parents had told them.

I wasn't saying a thing. Neither was Red. He was sitting on the couch. I was sitting on the rug against the bathtub. We were both waiting for Mr. Acevedo or Ms. Yvonne or Principal Darling, or anyone.

Finally, Mr. Acevedo appeared.

"Sorry I'm late," he said, standing in the doorway. "You'll understand why in a few minutes. Let's put our belongings away—if you have any today—and then we're all going to head down to Principal Darling's office."

"I didn't bring anything," Avery said, rolling past him. "I'll meet you there." She wheeled into the hall and headed for the elevator.

I popped to my feet. "I'm going with her," I said, darting for the door.

Mr. Acevedo always let someone ride the elevator with Avery, but the person had to ask permission, not *tell* Mr. Acevedo while he was racing by.

Except on the last day of elementary school. Evidently, the permission rule didn't apply on the last day of elementary school.

* * *

"You ever get stuck in an elevator?" I asked Avery as the door closed.

"Dude, you don't talk about getting stuck in an elevator when you're in an elevator," she said.

"We're only going one floor," I said.

"It doesn't matter."

"Did Diego ever tell you about bumper-vators?" I asked.

"What?" Avery curled her lip.

"Bumper-vators," I said. "Over Easter vacation, when Clifton United stayed at the hotel for the basketball—"

"You're doing that annoying thing again," she said, cutting me off. "I'm not in the mood for you."

"I'm just trying to make conversation, Avery."

"Whatever, dude," she said. "All I want to think about right now is Principal Darling's office."

The elevator doors opened, and Avery wheeled off. I followed and nearly walked right into her because she hockey-stopped as soon as she turned onto the main hallway. She glanced at me and then stared back down the hall.

We couldn't believe our eyes.

Everyone

Fifth-grade parents were streaming out of Principal Darling's office. I spotted Suzanne. Then I spotted Mom. We saw each other at the same time. She headed right for me.

"What's going on, Mom?" I asked.

"Where's the next closest staircase?" she said, walking up.

"The Book Stairs," I said, pointing down the hall. All the other parents were heading for the stairs directly across from the main office. "What's going on?"

"The meeting's been moved to your classroom," she answered.

"What meeting?" I asked as we started walking. "What's happening?"

"The school board went too far."

"It looks like everyone's parents are here," I said.

"Just about."

We turned onto the K-1 hallway, and when we reached

the Book Stairs, I held the door for Mom. We headed up the steps.

"What's going to happen?" I asked.

"We're about to find out," she said.

"Is the school board changing its mind?"

She stopped on the middle landing. "These parents aren't about to go quietly," she said. She touched my arm. "Yesterday, I told you I needed you to trust me on this."

"I know," I said. "I do."

"Good," she said. "When we're at the meeting now, I don't want you to say a thing. Not a word."

"Why not?"

"You're not going to say anything. I'm not going to say anything."

"You're not going to say anything?" I said. "Ha!"

She smiled. "Honey, if things go the way I think they will, I won't have to. Neither will you." She picked a piece of lint from my locks. "We had your backs the whole time."

"Who's 'we'?" I asked.

"The parents," she said. "Some of them wanted to step in on Wednesday when the board took away Gala25, but we convinced them not to."

"We or you?" I asked.

Mom smiled again.

"Ha!" I pointed. "I knew it."

"Honey, we were watching from a distance this whole week," she said. "We all had a pretty good idea how the district was going to respond, but we all agreed to let it happen."

"Why?"

"Honestly?" she said. "It was a good learning experience for you, and we were all so proud of the way you were organizing and mobilizing. It was a joy to watch." She tilted her head. "But when the board went after Mr. Acevedo and—"

"That is why he's leaving RJE," I interrupted. "I knew it!"

"When they went after him," Mom continued, "and then piled on with this middle school athletics nonsense, those were game changers. For all of us. Including me."

"But what about your school?" I asked. "And your district? What happens when they find out—"

"Don't worry about it," Mom said, cutting me off. "It doesn't concern you."

"You said it does."

"I was wrong."

I shook out my dreads and smiled. "Did Lesley Irving just admit she was—"

"No one messes with my kid." She cut me off again and spoke with an edge. "No one. Not like this. No way."

"Thanks, Mom."

She picked another piece of lint from my locks. "I can't

believe how ratty these are," she said. "We're taking care of them as soon as we get home tonight."

The Book Stairs door opened.

"Rip's Mom!" Red said, bounding up the stairs. "Hi, Rip's Mom. Hi, Mason Irving."

"Hello, Red," Mom said.

"We're going to the meeting in Room 208," Red said. Suzanne and Ms. Yvonne followed him up the steps. "Are you going to the meeting in Room 208?"

"We sure are," Mom said.

Red shook his fists next to his cheeks. "We can all go together," he said.

"That sounds like a terrific idea," Mom said.

I held out my fist to Red. "Strength in numbers," I said.

"Oh, yeah, Mason Irving." Red gave me a pound. "Strength in numbers."

* * *

Everyone was here.

Everyone.

The kids sat in the meeting area. I was on the carpet by the door between Avery and Red, who sat on the couch's armrest.

The grown-ups were at our tables, but there weren't enough seats. Some sat on the windowsill. The rest stood by the YO! READ THIS! board.

That's where Ms. Waldon and Mr. Goldberg, the head custodian, were. Mr. Goldberg was holding a copy of the Muhammad Ali biography I read earlier in the spring, the one I'd recommended on the board he was standing in front of. I thought back to the last T3. After Mr. Acevedo had finished reading, Mr. Goldberg told us he was taking a children's literature course over the summer, and in the fall he was starting night school so that he could earn a degree in early childhood education.

Ms. Yvonne, Mr. Acevedo, Ms. Wright, and Ms. Hamburger stood by the front closet.

Yes, that Ms. Wright and that Ms. Hamburger. When they walked into Room 208, the parents clapped. It was so strange seeing our teacher from last year, the teacher we were supposed to have this year, and the teachers we did have this year all standing together.

The Lunch Bunch—Ms. Eunice, Ms. Carmen, Ms. Joan, Ms. Audrey, and Ms. Liz—all stood by the Swag Corner. When they walked in, Red gave them each a hug, and when Red hugged Ms. Audrey, she started to cry. Red had never hugged her before. He'd never hugged any of the Lunch Bunch before.

Principal Darling stood against the whiteboard. She wasn't running this meeting. An assistant superintendent wearing a suit and tie and Edna Mode were. It was about to begin.

Everyone was here.

Everyone.

* * *

You know those town hall meetings you see on the news or TV shows where the moment the person running the meeting starts to say anything, someone in the audience interrupts or shouts them down?

This was one of those meetings.

"You picked on the wrong kids," Gavin's dad said as soon as Suit and Tie introduced himself.

"We want the names of the school board members who made this decision," Trinity's mom said. She pounded the windowsill. "We're not leaving until we have them."

"We're not leaving until their decision is reversed!" Christine's mom shouted.

Suit and Tie held up his hands. "I appreciate your—"

"I don't think you do," Attie's mom said, cutting him off. "You appreciate nothing."

"Here we go," Attie said with her hand cupped over her mouth. She was sitting in front of me on the rug. "Show-time."

"This school board is so far removed from reality," Attie's mom said, standing up. "Their handling of this situation was reckless and contrary to commonsense educational practices. They are not acting in the best interests of children. They've demonstrated they are unfit for office."

"Why don't you sit back down?" Attie's father said, reaching for her arm.

"Because I'm just getting started," she said. She pointed at Suit and Tie. "Do you fail to recognize the monumental stupidity of this school board's actions? First, they ban twenty-four kids from a school fund-raiser. But that's not banning twenty-four kids. That's banning twenty-four families and their friends. This is a fund-raiser. That's thousands and thousands of dollars for the school, for the kids. How shortsighted can they be?"

I peeked over at Attie. She was loving every word of this. I covered my smile.

"Then they tell our kids they can't play middle school athletics in the fall?" Attie's mom went on. "Where is the value in that? Who does that?" She motioned to the other parents. "We're prepared to do whatever it takes to make sure that doesn't happen."

"We're prepared to do whatever it takes to make sure Mr. Acevedo gets his job back," Diego's uncle said, standing up.

"I think everyone here needs to take a step back," Edna Mode said.

Diego's uncle didn't think so. "That man is a great teacher," he said, motioning to Mr. Acevedo. "I wish my Diego had a teacher like Mr. Acevedo every year. I wish every student in this district did. But this board wants to get rid of teachers like Mr. Acevedo, and we're not putting up with that."

I checked Diego. He was bobbing his head to his uncle's words and smiling like Red on a basketball court.

"To show we mean business," Diego's uncle went on, "we're prepared to hold our own graduation." He moved next to Attie's mom. "We're prepared to hold our own Gala25."

"That's right," Attie's mom said. "We've decided we're not letting you take away anything from our kids."

"We're not letting you take away *anything* from these kids either," Ms. Hamburger said.

Some of the parents clapped.

Ms. Hamburger stepped to Edna Mode and Suit and Tie. "I won't be attending Gala25," she said, "and I won't be attending graduation if all these decisions aren't reversed."

"That goes for me, too." Ms. Wright waved her hand.

"Same for us," Ms. Audrey said. She motioned to the Lunch Bunch. "We won't be there either."

Ms. Hamburger pointed to Mr. Acevedo. "For the last ten months, this young man has provided these students with an exceptional educational experience. He's shown them the importance of community, championed their voices, and encouraged them to be inquisitive."

I pumped a fist. No wonder everyone loved Ms. Hamburger. Ms. Hamburger was a boss.

"But that's not what you're telling them," she said, wagging her finger at Edna Mode and Suit and Tie. "You're telling them to be obedient. You don't want them to question. You don't want them to be curious."

Be curious.

Mr. Acevedo was always telling us curiosity was permitted in Room 208. Ms. Hamburger sounded an awful lot like Mr. Acevedo.

"What is happening here is not acceptable," Ms. Hamburger went on. "People need to know what you're doing. People need to know that you're harming children." She paused. "I'm the type of person who will make sure people know about what's going on here. So I strongly urge you to revisit these decisions."

I checked Mom. She sat at my table with her chin in her hand. She was right. She wasn't going to have to say a thing.

Red leaned down and tapped my shoulder. "Strength in numbers, Mason Irving," he said, holding out his fist.

I gave him a pound. "Strength in numbers."

Hoops Machine!

"Hey, what are you doing, kid?" Groll said angrily.

I kept on walking along the sideline and pretended not to hear him.

"I'm talking to you." Groll jumped into my path. "Let's go." He grabbed my arm. "You're coming with me."

As Groll pulled me onto the court, the Clifton High School gymnasium cheered. Dance music began to play. I chomped on my lip so that I didn't smile. My Hoops Machine dream was about to commence.

In the opening circle, they bounced the ball off my head harder than they usually did off their guest. Then they bounced the ball off my butt harder than usual. They pushed and shoved me harder, too.

They'd told me they were going to. They said they *needed* to since I missed the last practice and final walk-through. They said it would help keep me sharp and focused, but I wasn't buying it. Not for a second. They were messing with me, but I didn't mind. Not at all.

Now I stood between Ruiz and Croft and clapped as Sinanis did his behind-the-back, over-the-shoulder self-passing moves. We circled right as Rekate butt-spun in the middle and did her dribbling routine. We laughed and pointed as Bailey danced his Carlton.

"Good to have you back, Hoops Skywalker," Ruiz said. She bumped my shoulder. "You're up, you're up."

I backpedaled to the side-line and then faced the bleachers. I pumped both fists and pulled off my shirt, revealing my black-and-white Hoops Machine jersey.

The Clifton High School gym cheered louder.

"Oh, yeah, Mason Irving!" Red shouted.

With my basketball eyes, I spotted Red standing on the front row of the bleachers, twirling his head-phones.

"Ladies and gentlemen," Ruiz's voice boomed from the speakers, "introducing the newest member of Hoops Machine. Out of Reese Jones Elementary, wearing number twenty-four, our very own young Jedi warrior, Mason 'Rip' Irvingggggggg!"

I traced a path with my eyes back to the circle. I rocked in place and shook out my arms. Then I took off and sprinted for the middle.

I did a full flip and stuck the landing in the center of the Hoops Machine opening circle.

"Boo-yah!" I hammer-fisted the air.

Gersh passed me the ball, and I dropped to the floor. Move for move, I performed Rekate's seated dribbling routine and nailed her signature crossover. I popped to my feet and busted out the best Steph Curry spider-dribble I ever did. I followed that with my sickest broken-windshield-wiper dribbling, which included a ridiculous stop-on-a-dime, Rip Hamilton change of direction.

"Well done, well done," Ruiz said. She leaped into the middle of the circle. "Ladies and gentlemen," she announced, "let's hear it for Hoops Skywalker!"

The Clifton High School gymnasium stood and cheered. It was the loudest I ever heard it.

* * *

I didn't realize the Hoops Machine jerseys were reversible until Ruiz turned hers inside out. She told me, Bailey, and

Gersh to reverse ours, too. Croft took off his warm-up jacket. We were Team Black in the team scrimmage.

Groll, Sinanis, Rekate, Skeggs, and Mega-Man were Team White. They had the ball. Groll was bringing it up. I was guarding Skeggs, and just like in practice, I could already see she was looking for Mega-Man.

Mega-Man's dad was here. He made it! When he walked into the gym, he did need to use a cane, but he was here. Now he sat in the bleachers at center court, smiling like I'd never seen him smile before.

"Back screen, back screen!" Ruiz called.

I felt for Rekate's pick behind me.

Groll's pass went to Skeggs, and just like I anticipated, she touch-passed it to Mega-Man cutting down the lane, but the Gnat didn't jump into the lane and steal the ball.

The Gnat. That's my other nickname, and I *know* the origin of this one. It's what they called me on my third-grade select team because when I play defense, I can be incredibly annoying. Like a gnat.

But this time, the Gnat let the ball sail by. Mega-Man caught the pass and sank his layup.

"Yes!" Mega-Man basketball-smiled like Red and pumped his fists over his head. "Yes!"

The Clifton High School gymnasium cheered wildly.

Mega-Man's dad stood and raised his cane up and down.

"Way to go," I said, racing over and giving Mega-Man a pound.

"I'm so happy you're here, Rip," he said, patting my shoulder.

"You and me both," I said.

Michael Jackson's "Thriller" started to play over the speaker, and both teams formed a triangle at center court. Ruiz was at the point. Mega-Man and I were the other corners. In perfect sync, we performed the zombie dance.

As soon as the music ended, Croft brought the ball upcourt. "Here we go, Jedi," he said. "All eyes on you."

It was my turn now. I was in full-throttle basketball mode.

Croft wheeled across midcourt and underhanded a crisp pass to Ruiz on the far side. She dribbled toward the lane, and when she reached the paint, she fired the ball out to me. I sent it right back to her as she cut down the lane for the layup . . .

But that wasn't our set play.

I followed my pass, blew by Skeggs—who was guarding me—and charged into the paint. Ruiz's no-look, over-the-shoulder pass was waiting for me. I plucked it out of the air and sank my layup.

"Boo-yah!" Hoops Machine cheered.

"Time out!" Croft called. He wheeled to the sideline and hockey-stopped in front of Avery. "Avery Goodman?"

"Yeah?" she said.

Croft pulled off his jersey, turned it inside out, and tossed it to her.

Avery held it up. The name on the back wasn't Croft. It was Goodman. The uniform number was eleven.

"Let's go," Croft said, backward-rolling onto the court. He motioned with his head for her to join him. "Time to get your game on."

Avery slipped her bag off her chair and unlocked the brakes.

"You have to put on your jersey, Avery Goodman," Red said.

"Whatever, dude," she said.

"Yo, you do," Diego added.

Avery put on her jersey and wheeled out to Croft waiting at midcourt. Hoops Machine formed a wide circle around them and clapped rhythmically as they played catch. The Clifton High School gymnasium clapped along.

A few moments later, Croft motioned for Bray and Wicks to clear some space and then rolled next to Avery. "All eyes on you," he said, placing the ball in her lap. He pointed to the hoop.

Without hesitating, Avery began dribbling toward the basket. The clapping grew louder as she wheeled across the top of the key and down the lane. But a few feet from the hoop, she turned and headed for the corner.

I clasped my hands and pressed my thumbs and knuckles to my lips. I knew exactly what she was going to do.

C'mon, Avery. You got this. Make it. Make it.

Before she reached the three-point line, she spun around and faced the basket.

"Money!" she said as she took the shot.

Swish!

＊ ＊ ＊

"You ready, you ready?" Ruiz shouted from in front of the scorer's table.

Mega-Man raised his fist.

"You got this," I said. I stood right behind him along the baseline.

The Clifton High School gym stomped and clapped as "We Will Rock You" blasted from the speakers and Mega-Man got set to dunk for the HM Flyers.

Ruiz turned to the crowd and motioned for everyone to join in:

"On your mark, get set, go!"

Holding the basketball like a fullback, Mega-Man took off and charged downcourt. When he reached the mini trampoline in the paint, he jumped onto it with both feet and sprang into the air. With two hands, he dunked the basketball.

"Mega-Man, Mega-Man!" Ruiz chanted.

The HM Flyers greeted Mega-Man on the mat under the hoop like a baseball team greeted a player after a walk-off home run.

"Mega-Man, Mega-Man!" the crowd cheered.

Ruiz looked my way. "You ready, Hoops Skywalker?"

I shook out my arms and legs and stepped up to the baseline. I checked my friends sitting in the front row of the bleachers. Avery still had on her number eleven Hoops Machine jersey. Diego sat beside her with his arm resting on her shoulder. Red was on the other side of Avery. He was bouncing his knees and spinning his headphones around his wrist.

I looked back at Ruiz, and inside my head, I heard what she'd told me at the very first practice:

I'm digging the way you seizing the moment, Hoops Skywalker.

I raised my fist.

Ruiz turned to the audience.

"On your mark," everyone said, "get set, go!"

I power-dribbled once and then sprinted like a gymnast heading for a vault. I hurtled onto the trampoline and took off. Soaring through the air, I raised my arms, kicked out my legs, arched my back, and flew toward the hoop for a one-handed monster dunk.

"Boo-yah!"

* * *

For the community scrimmage, I was on Team White along with Ruiz, Groll, Skeggs, and Mr. Acevedo. Yeah,

Mr. Acevedo. For the first time, I was playing in a basketball game on the same team as my fifth-grade teacher.

"Let's make it count," he said, holding out his fists.

I gave him a double pound and smiled. "Luck equals preparation plus opportunity, right?"

"You know it."

I looked downcourt at Team Black—Bailey, Rekate, Gersh, Coach Lebo—the Clifton High School varsity basketball coach—and Lesley Irving.

That's right, my mom was playing. I had no idea she was going to be part of the scrimmage until she stepped onto the court.

"I'm coming for you," she said, pointing two fingers at her eyes and then pointing them at me.

"We'll see," I said, waving my hand.

"I got to play with Hoops Machine after all," she said.

"You're going to wish you didn't," I said, smiling.

We had the ball first. I was running the point.

"Irving brings up the ball," I play-by-played. "He's guarded by Bailey, who meets him at the time line. Dribbling left, Irving dishes to Acevedo and cuts toward Ruiz. Ruiz goes middle and gets the ball back from Acevedo. Bailey switches and picks him. Oh! Lesley Irving is now matched up with Mason Irving. We have a mother-son showdown on defense!"

Lesley Irving pointed her fingers at her eyes again and aimed them back at me.

"Right," I said.

I jab-stepped toward the top of the key. Mom took the bait and went for my fake. I Rip Hamilton–changed direction and broke for the hoop. Ruiz saw I had a step on Mom, but she didn't pass to me. Instead she sent the ball back to Mr. Acevedo, who then sent a no-look touch pass my way. I caught the ball under the basket and flipped it up for a layup.

I pointed my fingers at my eyes and then aimed them at Mom. But I wasn't done. Now it was time for the Gnat.

On defense, I picked up Bailey in the backcourt and denied him the ball. But for some reason, Coach Lebo still passed to him. Bad idea. I swarmed and stole the ball, and just like that, Mr. Acevedo and I had a two-on-one fast break. I led him with a one-handed bounce pass. He put up a floater, sank it, and got fouled in the act.

But instead of heading to the charity stripe to complete the three-point play, he headed for the sideline.

"You take my free throw?" he said to Red.

"Me?" Red pointed to himself.

"Of course." Mr. Acevedo pointed to the court. "You're the free-throw shooting machine."

"Oh, yeah!" Red hopped from foot to foot. He pulled

his headphones from around his neck and tossed them onto the bleachers. "Thanks, Mr. Acevedo."

"You'll need this." Mr. Acevedo took off his jersey and handed it to Red.

"Thanks, Mr. Acevedo," Red said again.

He put on the jersey and ran to the foul line.

The Clifton High School gymnasium stood and cheered.

With my basketball eyes, I spotted Suzanne. She had her hands cupped over her nose and mouth. Ms. Yvonne had her arm around her. Tears streamed from the corners of Suzanne's eyes.

At the foul line, Red trapped the ball soccer-style under his left foot and took several breaths. With both hands, he picked up the ball, squared his shoulders, and looked at the front rim. He dribbled three times low to the ground—hard dribbles—and then stood back up. He spun the ball until his fingers were right and then looked at the rim again. He extended his arms and took the shot.

Underhanded.

Swish!

* * *

"It's electric!" everyone shouted.

I do mean everyone. Everyone who'd been in the

bleachers was now out on the court with Hoops Machine. Everyone was dancing the Electric Slide.

"Boogie-woogie-woogie!" everyone sang.

"Electric Boogie" is one of those songs you've heard a gazillion times, but you still don't know the words. You only know two lines, and you say them even when you're not supposed to, but no one cares.

"It's electric!"

I was dancing next to Red. He was basketball-smiling and bumping into me every time we turned or changed direction. I'm pretty sure he was doing it on purpose.

We were dancing with all our classmates—Diego, Attie, Xander, Melissa, everyone. Mega-Man was with us, too. Avery was on the end next to Croft. They were both popping wheelies and doing three-sixties. Avery was still wearing her Hoops Machine jersey.

"Boogie-woogie-woogie!"

Each time we turned, my basketball eyes spotted Mr. Acevedo. Ms. Yvonne was on one side of him, Ms. Hamburger on the other. Ms. Wright was next to her. They were all doing their own version of the Electric Slide. Every time the rows turned, they danced in circles around one another.

Mom and Dana danced with Ms. Waldon, Mr. Goldberg, and the Lunch Bunch. Suzanne was between Ms.

Audrey and Ms. Liz. Mom was boogie-woogie-ing with Ms. Joan. Each time Mom spotted me, she waved with both hands.

I waved back.

Everyone was here. Everyone came through. Everything worked out.

"It's electric!"

Middle School!

At 7:25 on Sunday morning, I met Red at the end of his driveway, just like I did pretty much every weekday morning this year except for last week.

Today, Red was waiting for me with his elementary school graduation present, a black Labrador retriever puppy.

"You must be Ambi Turner," I said.

I bent down to greet her but stopped myself. This was

my first time meeting Ambi Turner. She needed to know I was the one in control. She needed to know I was the boss.

"Sit, Ambi Turner," I said firmly. I held out my hand palm up and raised it. "Sit."

She didn't respond.

"Here, Mason Irving," Red said. He handed me a few tiny pieces of carrot. "Ask her again, and when you do, move the carrot from in front of her nose to over her eyes. As soon as she sits, give her the carrot."

I did exactly as Red said. It worked.

"Good girl!" I bent down and rubbed her head. "Nice to meet you, Ambi."

"Good boy, Mason Irving." Red laughed.

I made a face. "Very funny," I said. I pressed my nose to Ambi's. "I can't wait for you to meet Bubba."

"Ambi Turner's not allowed to meet Bubba Chuck yet," Red said. "Ambi Turner's not allowed to meet other dogs for another few weeks."

"I can't wait for you to meet Bubba in a few weeks," I said, still rubbing my nose against Ambi's.

"I got a puppy for graduation, Mason Irving!" Red hopped from foot to foot and danced in a circle. "I got a puppy. I got a puppy."

"She's awesome."

"She's the awesomest!" Red said.

"You almost ready to go?" I asked.

"Almost," Red said. "I have to put Ambi Turner inside, but first, watch this."

Using the lead and the carrots, Red moved Ambi Turner so that she was sitting next to his right leg, brushing up against him. He stared at her eyes and waited for her to focus on him. As soon as she did, Red gave the lead a light tug, took a step forward, and turned her into him. They walked side by side toward the house. At the door, Red looked back and smiled.

"I have to make sure Ambi Turner can go left," he said. "I have to make sure Ambi Turner's an ambi-turner!"

* * *

We didn't have school today because it was Sunday. We also didn't have school today because we graduated. But since Red and I didn't get to walk to Reese Jones Elementary this past week like we always did, we decided one final walk was in order—Orleans Lane to Key Place to Niagara Drive.

"I have a basketball question," Red said as we headed down Key Place. "Who would you rather have on your team, Michael Jordan or LeBron James?"

"Michael Jordan," I answered instantly. "No doubt."

"Yeah, Michael Jordan," Red said. "Michael Jordan number one. LeBron James number two."

"No one will ever top MJ," I said.

"Do game two of the 1991 NBA Finals, Mason Irving," he said. "Bulls versus Lakers."

I knew exactly what he was talking about. I air-dribbled to the corner and turned around.

"The look-away to Levingston," I said, imitating Marv Albert's legendary play-by-play call. "Jordan." I then pretended to do MJ's high-flying, hand-switching layup. "Oh, a spectacular move by Michael Jordan!"

As we turned the corner onto Niagara Drive, I jumped up and swatted the stop sign with my fingertips. At the start of fifth grade, I couldn't touch it. Red spun around the stop sign like he always did.

"I can't believe we're in middle school," I said. "It's going to be so different."

"It's going to be so different," Red said.

I pulled a granola bar from my pocket, snapped off a piece, and tossed it to Red. "Are you nervous?" I asked.

"Nervous about what?"

"Middle school."

"Why would I be nervous about middle school?"

"I don't know."

"Are you nervous about middle school?"

I soccer-kicked a dandelion and watched the fluff float off. "A little," I said.

"Why are you nervous?"

I shrugged. "I don't know."

"Don't worry." Red patted my shoulder. "No one will mess with Mason Irving while I'm around."

I laughed. "Thanks, Red."

Up ahead, we could see the entrance to the schoolyard. We walked faster.

We reached the gate to the schoolyard, but since I didn't have my backpack, I pretended to slip it off my shoulders and fling it over the chain-link fence. Red grabbed the metal post, spun around it, and made like he caught the bag by the straps.

"Boo-yah!" I hammer-fisted the air.

"Bam!" Red held up the imaginary backpack.

We zigzagged through the portables—the second- and third-grade classrooms—and raced for the playground. We stopped at the entrance.

"One last obstacle course?" I said.

"Oh, yeah," Red said. "One last obstacle course."

I shook out my hair and brushed back the locks above my ears. "You ready?"

"Ready as I'll ever be, Mason Irving."

My eyes traced the path to the balance beam. I rocked in place and shook my arms. "On your mark," I said, "get set . . ."

"Go!"

I took off first and did a full flip, sticking the landing a couple feet in front of the balance beam. Red bolted for the monkey bars. I darted for the climbing wall. I made like Spider-Man, pulled myself to the upper deck, and then leaped all the way across to the spiral slide, where Red was waiting. We traded a fist bump and then dove for the slide. Red went down first. I followed right behind him. When we both reached the sand, we hammer-fisted the air.

"Boo-yah!"